SURVIVAL IN THE MOUNTAINS

CARRIE STUART PARKS

LOVE INSPIRED SUSPENSE
INSPIRATIONAL ROMANCE

Recycling programs for this product may not exist in your area.

ISBN-13: 978-1-335-95779-5

Survival in the Mountains

For questions and comments about the quality of this book, please contact us at CustomerService@Harlequin.com.

Love Inspired
22 Adelaide St. West, 41st Floor
Toronto, Ontario M5H 4E3, Canada
www.LoveInspired.com

HarperCollins Publishers
Macken House, 39/40 Mayor Street Upper,
Dublin 1, D01 C9W8, Ireland
www.HarperCollins.com

Printed in Lithuania

Bethany raced to Joshua's prone body on the cabin floor. She gently turned him over.

He opened his eyes and stared at her, at first blankly, then with recognition.

"What did they do to you?"

Joshua reached for the back of his head, winced, then looked at his hand, now covered in blood. "One of the goons must have been waiting for me outside." He glanced at the door. "Is it...?"

It was locked. Bethany's dog, Izzy, made her way to the door, sniffing under it. Bethany ran from window to window. Plywood had been nailed over each one. "Looks like they want us to stay put."

Outside, some clinking sounds penetrated.

Izzy barked.

They all looked toward the door. The small crack underneath now glowed.

A slender tongue of flame whispered, then crept higher, snapping at the air. In seconds, it climbed the door, multiplying and spreading with terrifying speed...

Carrie Stuart Parks is an internationally known forensic artist and law enforcement instructor, working on major criminal cases throughout the nation. Mentored by her friend Frank Peretti, she has written bestselling mystery/suspense novels that have won numerous awards, including several Christys and Carols. Married to fellow fine and forensic artist, Rick, they make their home on the family ranch in the mountains of North Idaho.

Books by Carrie Stuart Parks

Love Inspired Suspense

Escaping the Wilderness
Survival in the Mountains

Visit the Author Profile page at LoveInspired.com.

Wherefore seeing we also are compassed about with so great a cloud of witnesses, let us lay aside every weight, and the sin which doth so easily beset us, and let us run with patience the race that is set before us.

—*Hebrews* 12:1

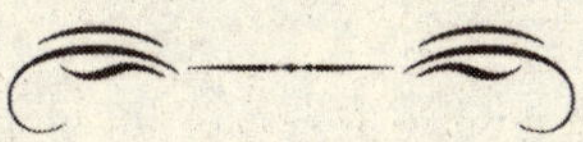

To Lynette, my dear friend. Thank you.

ONE

Pain radiated through her skull, sharp and relentless. She tried to open her eyes, but something held them glued shut. Intense heat lapped at her side. Somewhere a wailing howl pounded her eardrums. The stench of burning rubber clogged her nostrils. Bile burned the back of her throat. Darkness swirled around her brain.

Strong, calloused hands latched on to her wrists, prying them free from the steering wheel she'd been clutching. She was dragged sideways, shards of glass digging into her ribs and hip, tearing cloth and skin. She screamed. Her legs caught on something and she was yanked harder. Her arms felt like they were dislocating from her shoulders. She screamed again, harder.

The darkness won. She embraced the nothingness, drifting gently, then jostling and bumping up and down. She wanted to protest the rough treatment, but her mouth was no longer a part of her body.

She was now flying, rising up, then lowering. She was as light as air. Maybe she *was* air. She needed to see where she was. She opened her eyes, then blinked.

Log walls encased a room with a cedar ceiling and lit with a warm, golden glow. A fire crackled in a river stone fireplace.

That wasn't right. Didn't you have to fly outside? Logic evaded her and her head thumped in pain.

A wave of nausea struck. She closed her eyes and concentrated on not vomiting.

Noise came from her right. Sounds that hurt her ears. She wanted to curl up on her side and make the sound and the pain go away.

Inky darkness swirled around her. She could just embrace it, dive into its depths.

"Wake up."

The voice pushed through the black fog.

"Wake up, lady."

"No," she whispered. "Go 'way."

"Lady, I need you to open your eyes."

Open her eyes? "No." Her voice was louder.

"If you don't open your eyes, I'll have to open them for you. I need to see if one pupil is larger than the other."

That didn't make sense. Nothing made sense. She wanted to sleep off this groggy feeling.

"Lady—"

She opened her eyes to make him stop talking. Two men stood above her, both holding the handset of a phone. She blinked and the two men merged into one.

"Yeah, Doc," the man spoke into the phone. "They seem to be the same size." He listened for a moment. "Gotcha." He looked down at her. "What's your name?"

Name? She pondered the question. Did she have a name? Did she even need one? "I don't know."

"She doesn't remember," he said into the phone, then nodded at whatever was being said. "Right. Okay. We'll be… Doc? Dr. Wallace? Hello? Hello… ?" He turned away.

She closed her eyes, but the room spun around her before settling into a gentle rocking. She opened them again.

The man had moved from the bed… Bed! She felt the crisp sheets under her fingers.

An odd huffing sound came from beside her. She carefully turned her head, not wanting to launch the nausea, dizziness or pain.

A dog sprawled next to her, snoring gently. Not a dog. Her dog. "Izzy," she whispered.

The dog looked up, then shifted so her large head was across her midsection.

"Did you say 'Izzy'?" The man returned to her side.

"Yes. My dog, Izzy." She stroked the dog's head.

"You remember your dog's name, but not yours?"

"No."

"The doctor said your memory might be spotty at first. He thinks it will all—or mostly—come back to you."

She frowned at him. "What's your name?"

"Joshua. I pulled you from the fire. Do you remember the fire? The car accident?"

"No. I was in an accident?"

Joshua pulled a chair next to the bed, then glanced at his watch. "Your car went over a cliff. I heard the crashing and rode over to check it out. The car had started to burn and you were still inside with your dog. Do you remember any of that?"

She closed her eyes to concentrate, then immediately opened them to chase away the tilt-a-whirl in her brain. The fire, lapping flames reaching for her skin. She shuttered the images. She now noticed the rancid odor around her. And the lesser smell of… "Horse?"

He scratched his chin and looked at his watch again. "I was on horseback and brought you here to get my truck. Still no memory?"

The fog was slowly lifting, though her head still pounded. She started to shake her head, then muttered, "No." She concentrated on her rescuer.

He sat in profile to her. He had brown, almost black hair in need of a haircut, thick eyebrows, and skin roughened by the weather. It was hard to gauge his age, but she'd guess a few years older than her. A dark, five-o'clock shadow somewhat blurred his strong jawline.

"It sounds like you rescued Izzy and me from a terrible death. Thank you, Joshua."

He ducked his head. "Not gonna let you burn. But we have a slight problem."

She struggled to sit up, but gave up when the bed started spinning. "What?" She became aware of the growing odor of fire.

"Seems that fire that started in your car has launched a forest fire."

"But…how…oh!"

"I called the forest service, then the doctor. The line's now down, so we're cut off at the moment. I'll try a different way out. I hope." His last words were almost to himself.

The sick feeling from her head injury transferred to a heavy weight in her chest. "What does that mean, 'cut off'?"

He straightened in his chair. "Not a lotta roads around here. In fact, just one road in or out. Fire makes it that much harder. I'm going—" He looked up when a distant sound, like a large engine, permeated the room.

Izzy lifted her head and glanced toward the door.

Joshua stood and moved away.

She gingerly turned her head and tracked him with her gaze.

He strolled across the dimly lit cabin, opened the door and stared out before walking outside and closing the door behind him.

The roar grew louder along with the distinctive *wap, wap, wap* of a large helicopter. The aircraft seemed to fly directly over the cabin, rattling the walls and sending Izzy into a frenzy of barking. It sounded like they'd moved to the tarmac of a major airport.

The noise hurt her ears and added fuel to her headache.

As the cacophony continued, Joshua returned inside. "Something's off." He approached the bed where she could see him clearly.

He was wearing a plaid shirt, blue jeans, and had a set of

dog tags around his neck. He looked like the movie star Clive Owen but with one major difference.

A jagged, angry red scar ran down the left side of his face.

The woman's eyes widened slightly.

Joshua ducked his head to the side. *When will I ever learn?* "So…it appears the forest service is already using a helibucket and at least one tanker to put out the fire." He turned toward the kitchen. "Gotta get out of here. The wind could shift. You need water?" He glanced at her, expecting to see the usual look of pity in her eyes. Instead, they glittered with unshed tears. "What? Is something—"

"No. No. You've been so kind to me. You practically saved my life—no, you did save my life. I am so, so sorry if I offended you."

He turned toward her. "Are you always this nice?"

"How would I know?" she said sarcastically, then touched her mouth. "Apparently not. It would seem that I have a snarky side."

He snorted.

"I'll have some water," she said. "And what's off?"

"I don't follow."

"When you first came in, you said 'something's off.' What's off?"

He strolled to the kitchen, retrieved a bottle of water, then brought it to her before answering. "Do you know where you are?"

"Um. I think… Idaho?"

"Good. What do you know about the state?"

She chewed her lip. "I think…um…over sixty percent of Idaho is owned by the federal government and much of it is left in its primitive state. Is that right?"

"Yes."

"It seems strange that I can remember things like that and not my own name."

"As I said earlier, the doctor said your memory could come back in chunks. You're doing fine. Now, what do you know about wildfires?"

Her face reddened slightly and she carefully propped up on her pillow. "The…the US Forest Service is charged with caring for the federal lands. Their psychology before the late 1960s was to put out wildfires as soon as possible, not realizing that fires were a part of God's plans for a healthy ecosystem—"

"Do you believe in God?"

She was silent for a moment. "I think…no, I know I do. Just like I know Izzy's name."

The dog lifted her head at her name and she stroked it.

He resisted the urge to give her a reassuring hug. He was again struck with how lovely she was, with flawless skin currently smudged with soot, reddish-brown hair French-braided to below her shoulders, and blue-green eyes.

"You were saying?" She prodded him.

"Do you remember the Yellowstone fire?"

She started to shake her head, winced, then said, "No."

"After the devastating wildfire in Yellowstone Park in 1988, the forest service realized fires were natural and, unless the fire threatened homes or structures, for the most part they allowed them to burn. A tanker and a helibucket are a lot of resources for the fire out here."

She slowly nodded. "Maybe they're protecting you? This cabin?"

"I doubt it. But the road might be cleared."

The glass in her hand shook slightly. "Are we in any danger?"

"Let's just say that while you were drifting in and out of consciousness, I packed the pickup. I'll take you to the hospital—"

"No."

"You have a head injury and need to be checked out."

"I'm fine. Except for a headache and holes in my memory."

He really didn't have time to argue her decision. Forest fires were dangerous. "We'll talk about this later. Ready to move?"

"I guess we'll find out." She straightened, then pulled the sheet and blanket off her legs. The soot from her clothing had smudged his white sheets. "I'm sorry—"

"Don't be." He put out his hand to help her up.

She stood, then started to crumple.

In one smooth motion he picked her up. "So much for running a marathon today." He'd already packed the hiking boots she'd been wearing in the truck. He whistled for Izzy to follow and headed outside.

"Is this how you got me from my car to here?"

"Not quite." He nodded toward the horse trailer hitched to his truck. "Both of us rode Horse." He placed her on the passenger seat, then boosted Izzy next to her. "Fasten your seat belt." He shut the door, checked the hitch and trailer one last time, gave Horse a scratch on the rump, and got into the driver's seat.

"Horse? The name of your horse is Horse?"

"Simple, descriptive and accurate. Beats Izzy for a name." He started the engine, then pulled forward, keeping the grin off his face.

"Izzy is a great name. She's a bull terrier. Her full name is Isadora. Get it? *Is-adora-bull*. Get it?"

He winced. "Unfortunately." He eased onto the forest service road. Thick yellow smoke enveloped them and clogged their nostrils. "The doctor said this would happen." He nearly shouted to be heard over the steady roar of airplanes and helicopters overhead.

"What would happen? I'd make you wince with my puns?"

"Your memory returning." He glanced over at her. She was clutching the door with a white-knuckled grip. "What's wrong?"

"What?"

"I asked if something was wrong." He nodded toward her hand.

"What if the rest of my memory never comes back? My identification no doubt burned up in my car. Maybe I'm married?" She glanced at her hand. "No. No ring. Do you think someone will start to miss me? Worry? Call the police? The police! Shouldn't you call them?"

"Whoa. Take a deep breath. The accident just happened. Nothing's been called in. Do you always talk so much?"

"I have no idea. It seems to come naturally."

His laugh came out like more of a bark. "So, you're snarky, pragmatic and prone to bad puns."

"So it would seem. And you don't like to talk much, I gather."

He gave a half shrug. "Can't call without a cell. Do you see a cell tower?"

She looked around, then at him. "Oh."

"So, no cell towers, no cell service, and that leaves the dead landline or a satellite phone, which I don't have. We need to find a phone at the nearest big city."

"Are we near Boise?"

"Orofino." He worked on keeping a straight face. His life these past few years, since his accident that left him so scarred, had been quiet and solitary as an undercover officer for the Idaho Department of Fish and Game. He wasn't used to talking so much and he *really* wasn't used to a female sitting next to him in his pickup. An attractive, snarky, pragmatic and funny female at that.

"You know, Joshua…" Her voice cut into his musing. "You know everything about me…well, at least as much as I know, but I don't know anything about you. Outside of the whole 'knight in shining armor' saving my life."

He concentrated on driving. "Not much to know."

"Job? Family? Hobbies? Favorite song?"

"Working. None local. None. 'Amazing Grace.'" He gave her a sideways glance.

Her mouth was open. She shut it. "Elaborate. See? I can be as short in my language as you."

"I work on my ranch. I have a brother. I don't have a hobby. And 'Amazing Grace' has always been my favorite song. I'd ask you the same, but you won't remember."

She was silent for a moment. "Why are you helping me?" she asked in a quiet voice.

"To paraphrase Romans 15:1, being strong, I have an obligation to help those who are weak. The small print adds, 'This includes damsels in distress.'" He glanced at her again. "Besides, I'm just driving you to get help. That's all."

The smoke was clearing and patches of cobalt sky appeared. They drove for a few miles, the sounds of the aircraft diminishing. They were close to where her car flew off the road. *Will she notice?*

They came around a corner and the evidence of the fire was hard to miss. A scorched black slash of burned hillside stretched from one side of the road to the other. Wisps of white smoke still rose from different spots. The smell of burnt wood filled the air.

She gave an audible gasp. "I know this place."

His pulse quickened. "Yes. Your car went off the road here."

"No. I mean I remember…something."

"What?"

"The truck." Her voice trembled. "It smashed into my car, right here. It wasn't an accident. Someone tried to kill me."

He slammed on the brakes, the truck skidding to a sudden stop. "What?"

Her heart pounded, already racing from the fragmented memory surfacing in her mind. "I was driving here because…" She paused, the words catching in her throat. "Because… I don't know. But I remember there was a truck. A big black truck. It came out of nowhere, speeding up behind me. I thought it was trying to pass, so I slowed down and moved over, but…" Her voice wavered. The next fragment of memory slammed into her, vivid and raw. "It rammed into my bumper. My car spun out…"

She gasped as the memory overwhelmed her—spinning, the shriek of tires, the violent plunge off the road. Dirt, brush, trees blurred past in a chaotic whirl. Her own screams echoed in her ears, reverberating with the terror of the crash—

A hand touched her arm, warm and steady, grounding her.

The memory dissolved like fog, replaced by Joshua's face, his eyes locking onto hers with steady reassurance. "You're safe now."

Her chest heaved as she fought for calm. For the first time since waking up, she exhaled a little of the tension that had gripped her. "*B*. Bonny. Betty…no."

"You think your name starts with a *B*?"

"That's what seems to feel right."

"Barbara? Bailey? Bridget?"

She shook her head after each name.

"Belle? Beth—"

"Wait. Beth. Almost…" Her brain felt as if the haze was clearing. "Bethany," she murmured, her voice steadier than she expected. "My name is Bethany."

A truck, painted the distinctive green of the forest service, rumbled around the corner, stopping next to them.

Joshua rolled down his window as the driver sauntered over. "Hey, there," the ranger said, then squinted at Joshua. "You're Joshua McGregor, right?"

Joshua nodded.

"Thought so. People told me about your…um, you." He glanced at the back of Joshua's pickup, then at the horse trailer. He opened his mouth to speak, but his words were swallowed up by the enormous air tanker that flew low over the ridge above them, its shadow skimming the trees. Both men watched it until it disappeared over the next mountain.

Joshua raised an eyebrow, then jerked a thumb at the receding aircraft.

"Crazy," the ranger said. "By the time we'd identified and outlined the fire, two tankers and a helibucket were already on it. They pretty much contained, then knocked the fire out."

"Why is that crazy?" Bethany asked.

"It's not us." The ranger leaned against the truck. "Course, we're grateful for the help. The fire would have been a whole lot worse if they hadn't jumped on it."

"Who?" Joshua asked.

"Some private outfit with land in the area. Big money, looks like. Maybe one of those Hollywood types who own property in Idaho—Bruce Willis, Hanks, Eastwood, who knows? Anyway, fire's out. You're clear to head home if you want. We'll still look into what started it, but you and the missus are safe."

Bethany was about to offer information about the start of the fire and her status with Joshua when he shot her a quick frown and a jerk of his head. He turned his attention back to the ranger.

"Thanks. Good to know."

The ranger tapped the door twice, turned, and ambled back to his service truck.

Joshua waited until the truck had disappeared before putting his own vehicle into gear.

"Why didn't you want me to tell him about the accident?" Bethany asked.

"Not sure. But something's wrong." He pulled forward until they reached a split in the road, making it wide enough to turn around.

A shiver ran up Bethany's spine. "Wait, Joshua."

Joshua stopped the truck, then turned to look at her.

She rubbed her arms with a sudden chill. Something about this area was familiar. But what? She rolled down the window, letting in the tang of pine. Ponderosas surrounded the dirt and gravel road. A trickle of a stream on her right dropped down a tiny waterfall, its sound too loud, as if the forest held its breath. Next to the stream was a large cedar with a rusty and bent No Hunting sign nailed to the trunk. "That sign. I was to watch for it...but why?" Her voice was barely a whisper.

"Should we turn here?"

"That makes sense."

Joshua turned off the main forest service road to the smaller lane. The road climbed a gentle slope, then snaked around a series of switchbacks before entering a clearing. A small cabin, its weathered logs darkened by time and shadows, squatted in the center. The faint scent of mold and old smoke drifted toward her. Joshua turned the truck and trailer around before stopping the engine. He stared at the cabin. "Look familiar?"

Bethany stared at the log building, waiting for something to come back. A small memory tickle that she couldn't quite grasp whirled inside her brain. Was this a good place, or had something bad happened? She unsnapped the seat belt and opened the door.

"Wait. Let me help you."

She slid from the truck, briefly holding on to the side to steady her suddenly wobbly legs. "I'm okay." She let go and moved toward the cabin. The door was slightly ajar. She stopped. "Joshua?"

"Yeah. I see it." He'd come up behind her and stood next to her. He was fully a foot or more taller than her, something she hadn't noticed before. She knew he was physically strong from the ease with which he'd carried her to the car, but now he seemed downright fearless. "I don't like it." He frowned. "But maybe they evacuated."

"I don't believe it and neither do you. You don't leave your door open."

The door squeaked slightly in the breeze.

Izzy trotted past them on her stubby legs. Before Bethany could call her back, she entered the building.

"You wait here—"

But Bethany was already on the move, racing as fast as she could manage after her dog. "Izzy, Izzy come!" She crossed the lopsided porch and pushed the door fully open.

The gloomy interior of the cabin swallowed both Bethany and her dog.

Joshua tore after her, stopping just past the threshold, his eyes adjusting to the gloom.

Bethany stood frozen in the middle of the single room holding a piece of pink fabric. Her face had drained of color and she swayed slightly.

In two steps he was beside her, reaching for her to keep her from falling.

She clutched his arm. "This scarf belongs to my sister, Ruth. We came here… I drove here to visit my Aunt Nan."

"Maybe they left to get away from the fire?" The words rang hollow even to his own ears. The details didn't fit—the door of the 1950s-style refrigerator stood slightly ajar, drawers hung open as if rifled through in haste, and a spoon lay abandoned on the plank floor under the table. Each detail seemed to whisper a story left unfinished. "The truck that drove me off the road. Maybe they went here and…" She clenched her jaw.

"Let's not leap to conclusions just yet. Keep looking."

Bethany walked to the corner of the room where a faded calico curtain concealed a closet. On the floor sat a new pink suitcase. She knelt, flipped the latches and opened it. Neatly folded women's clothing spilled out. "This is my sister's suitcase. We were going to stay a few days. That's right. I remember." She rocked back on her heels. "If they were trying to get out before the fire reached them, why wouldn't she take her already packed suitcase?" She looked up at Joshua, her eyes pleading for a reasonable explanation. "This doesn't make sense."

Joshua couldn't meet her gaze. He had no reasonable answer. "Keep looking," he said gruffly.

He moved to the first of two small bedrooms. Twin beds were neatly made up with handmade quilts and an old trunk between them holding a copper lamp. Light came dimly through the only window and the room smelled faintly of moth balls. The second bedroom had a double bed also covered with a green-and-brown quilt. This room had a bureau containing women's clothing as did the closet. He had no way of telling if anything was missing.

In the corner rested a wooden desk with an incongruent modern light. Next to it was an industrial beige, two-drawer, metal filing cabinet.

He moved closer and squatted next to the desk, eyeing the surface. He could just make out a very slight dust-free pattern—the distinct shape of a mousepad, keyboard and computer. The desk drawers held only pens and a stray paperclip. The filing cabinets were also empty.

No sign of haste. The removal of the electronics had been methodical. His shoulders tightened and he stood. If she had a computer, she'd need a router. Would they have figured that out? He looked around the room. Routers were usually tucked out of sight. He went back to the closet, this time feeling on the top shelf. He quickly found the router.

"Joshua?"

Bethany's voice sounded strained.

He returned to the living room. She stood in front of a closet that had obviously been used as a pantry. A tin of coffee, box of tea bags, bottles of food coloring and vanilla, plastic containers of sugar and flour, and a number of soup cans stood on the otherwise barren shelves. "What?"

"My aunt sold jelly or jam or something like that. She had

quite a few jars in here. I saw them when I dropped off Ruth. They were going to have scones or something while I was… why did I leave?" She rubbed her forehead, then winced. "Okay. So. I left because… I was going… I don't know." She clenched her teeth.

He wanted to give her a reassuring hug, but he wasn't sure of her reaction. "Don't worry about it. It will come to you. Maybe we should consider going to the hospital—"

"Not with my sister and aunt missing. I need to find them."

He sighed. He needed to add *stubborn* to her description. "Did your aunt do work on a computer?"

She furrowed her brows at him. "I don't know. Why?"

"There was one on the desk but it's gone. So are any files she might have had."

Izzy was sniffing around the room. She stopped, looked up at Bethany, and gave her a toothy, open-mouthed grin.

This gave Joshua an idea. "If you let your dog sniff your sister's scarf, do you think your dog could track her?"

"That's a terrific idea—if Izzy had even the tiniest tracking genes." She squatted next to Izzy. "See this large head? It's all bone. No brains. Bull terriers are clowns, couch potatoes and lovable conversation starters." She hugged the dog. "She has a vocabulary of two words—her name and 'cookie.'"

The dog stopped panting, perked up her ears and stared at Bethany with her tiny eyes.

"I'm going to look around outside." Joshua made his way outside, then did a swift circuit of the house. Places like this, tucked back into the mountains, were often used for moonshiners or others on the edge of the law. The land dropped off sharply behind the cabin. Beside the structure, he found the satellite dish attached to the house, a pump house, an umber-brown old barn with an older Ford pickup, and a garage with a Carmel Edition Range Rover. The keys were on the seat.

He stared at the SUV. *None of this adds up.*

"Is that her car?"

Joshua jerked at the voice. He hadn't heard Bethany come up behind him. "Yeah. How rich is your aunt?"

"Rich? As far as I know, not at all. I mean, she sold jelly at the local festivals." She blinked at him, then studied the SUV.

Sunlight through the wide-spaced boards of the garage wall dappled the satin bronze finish. The windows were dark-tinted, making it difficult to see into the interior. In the quiet of the garage, the buzz of a fly seemed abnormally loud. *No. Heavenly Father, don't let it be a body...* Before he could move, Bethany leaped forward and jerked the rear door open.

TWO

Bethany held her breath, unable to move.

The car was empty.

She didn't know whether to scream, cry or drop to her knees and thank God.

Joshua gently pried her hand off the door handle. "Well, if your aunt isn't rich, what's she doing with a three-hundred-and-fifty-thousand-dollar, limited-edition SUV?"

He didn't seem to expect an answer. He'd already opened the passenger door and was rummaging through the glove box. He straightened, shut the doors, then walked around the car. He glanced at Bethany and quickly strolled outside.

She followed, catching a glimpse of him as he disappeared into the barn. By the time she caught up with him, he was inspecting an old blue Ford truck, sun-striped by the light poking through the barn's side. Hay dust twirled in the sunbeams.

"What is it?" she asked.

He looked up from his inspection. "No license plates. No vehicle title or insurance cards. Do you know if your aunt had any other form of transportation?"

A prickly chill ran up her spine. She shook her head. "There wasn't anything parked outside when I drove up." The words were out before she had a chance to think. *Maybe that's the secret to my memory. Just don't think.*

Joshua put his hands on his hips and looked up blankly. "Okay, then."

A whole host of weird, random thoughts ran through her head. *Abducted by space aliens. Slid through a time warp. Popped into another dimension.* The stuff of comic books and 1950s sci-fi movies. "There..." Her voice came out high and strained. She cleared her throat. "There has to be a reason they're gone. Maybe a neighbor dropped by and took them to town. Or they went for a walk in the woods. Or...something."

"Those are logical, but they don't fit the evidence." He raked a hand through his thick hair. "We'll figure it out."

His calm response felt like a soothing cup of chamomile tea. "Okay. What do you want me to do?"

He gave her an approving nod and her face warmed. "I suspect we'll need to report this to the sheriff, but before we do, we need to do one more sweep. We've already checked the house and outbuildings."

She turned and walked outside, then stood still and carefully looked around. The scent of fire still hung in the air but was slowly dissipating in the slight breeze. The cabin was in the middle of a clearing, surrounded by a thick wall of pines. Above the trees, blue-green mountains paraded into the distance. The dirt driveway circled around in front of the house with the remains of a rock-rimmed herbal garden in the middle. Joshua had parked the truck and trailer so it was pointed downhill toward the main road.

The tire impressions of their vehicle were etched into the dusty road, in places overlaying the tracks of her car. If someone had driven here after her but before Joshua's truck, those marks should have also shown up. "I don't see tracks besides ours and my car." She glanced over at Joshua.

He was staring at her, his expression unreadable. He looked away. "Good."

She rubbed her left hand, feeling for the engagement ring that had rested there so many months ago—the same ring her sister now wore. The ring— *Wait!* How had that memory slipped into her mind? She pressed to remember more. She'd been engaged. To...to... But no name or face came with that realization, only the words she must have repeated to herself. *Never again. Shattered trust doesn't mend,* followed by the scent of something earthy, sweet and tart.

"What happened? Your face changed just now. Did you remember something?"

She wasn't about to mention engagements, rings, a faceless fiancé, or ugly thoughts. She took a deep breath and instead said, "I was just wondering if it was good that I noticed no tire tracks or good there aren't any?"

His expression grew skeptical, but he just snorted, then slowly walked around the edge of the drive staring down. At one point he knelt. "Here."

"Here what?"

"Do you always question everything? Never mind. I know your answer." He stood.

She trotted over to him.

He pointed toward the trees on his right. "People walked here recently."

"How can you tell?"

He raised one eyebrow.

"Point made."

He turned toward the indicated path, but not before she spotted the twitch of a suppressed grin. She liked that. Maybe she could actually make him smile. She followed him single file to the tree line. He pushed the low-hanging branches aside, revealing a game trail. "How do you know people, not deer or elk, walked through here—oh."

He pointed to the clear outline of a man's shoe before continuing forward. The trail plunged through the thick pines, the sunlight blocked by the dense canopy overhead, and the temperature dropped. Joshua held branches aside to keep them from snapping backward into her face as they walked in deeper. They reached a small stream where Izzy nosily drank the clear water.

"Is that normal?" Joshua waved at the dog.

"Yes." *Now I'm giving short answers.* As he scanned the trees she leaned against a tree trunk, grateful for the support. Her head still thumped and the world tilted occasionally. "Joshua, what do you think happened?"

"That's what we're going to find out." He started down the trail at a good clip. She had to trot to keep up.

Ahead, the trail lightened, with dappled sunlight spotlighting their path. They burst through the trees into a clearing surrounded by sparsely spaced evergreens. Joshua crossed to the center and looked around.

Bethany caught up, slightly winded from the fast pace.

Joshua caught her attention. "Helicopter." He jerked his head at the flattened bushes, the parallel tracks packed into the grass.

Bethany's stomach clenched. "Shouldn't we call the sheriff?"

Joshua stared sightlessly at the distant mountains. "Yes, but do we have an abduction or someone missing after fleeing a fire?"

She had to admit his deep voice calmed the jittery feeling in her stomach.

"There's no sign of a struggle. No blood." He gave her a quick glance. "The fire could have caused them to take off, but…"

"But you think it's something else."

He gave a slow nod. "This aunt of yours. Tell me about her."

"I don't know much."

"I realize you're still struggling to remember—"

"That too, but I don't think I knew her well before we came to visit."

The sun had started to dip behind the mountains, tingeing the trees with a coral glow and casting long shadows in the valley.

"It's getting late. By the time we stop off at the cabin, drop off the trailer, let all the critters out—"

"Critters?"

"Horse, the cow, some chickens—"

"Right."

"Anyway, by the time we do that and try to get to town, it's going to be the middle of the night. Sheriff won't do anything before morning."

"Are we that far from town?"

Joshua scratched the black five-o'clock shadow on his cheek. "Not so much a question of distance. More like bad roads. Anyway, hopefully by morning, you'll have recovered more of your memory."

She bent down and hugged Izzy. "But I'm getting the feeling it's gonna be bad. Very bad," she whispered.

Joshua turned on his headlights and navigated down the driveway. The aunt's place was puzzling to say the least, and he was sure Bethany was remembering more than she let on. She'd stared at her hand strangely, but when pressed, brushed it off. *Why am I even involved?* He could drop off his horse and trailer, then drive her straight to town. She'd be there first thing in the morning to report to the sheriff.

He glanced over at her.

She was absently stroking her dog tucked between her feet and staring ahead.

She wouldn't have any money to get a motel room for the night. He'd have to book the room and give his name and identification.

That won't work.

He'd worked too hard on his cover as a reclusive mountain man to blow it now over a woman. They thought of him as one of them, a fugitive from justice, avoiding civilization.

If they found out he had a female with him—one he cared enough about to get a motel room for—they might see her as someone they could use against him. Possibly a weakness they could exploit. These men would stop at nothing to protect their lucrative industry.

So far, he'd managed to identify some of the poachers, but

they were low on the food chain. He needed to find the one arranging the sale of rare animal pelts to foreign markets.

And as for being seen going into the sheriff's department to support Bethany's story—that would end his undercover work on the spot. She'd have to convince the sheriff on her own that she wasn't some crazy person.

He could imagine the conversation with the sheriff.

"What's your name?" the sheriff would ask.

"Bethany."

"Bethany what?"

"I don't know."

"Where are you from, Bethany?"

"I don't know."

The sheriff would lean back and study her. "I see. What are you doing here?"

"I'm here because my sister and aunt are missing."

"What are their names?"

"Ruth and Aunt Nan."

"Last names?"

"I don't know."

The sheriff would dismiss her report before she even got to the strange circumstances they'd found at the cabin.

On the other hand, if her aunt and sister were really in trouble, the longer they waited, the worse it could be for them. His mind ping-ponged over the situation he was in.

Just enjoy her company while it lasts.

He jerked slightly at the thought. He hadn't thought he was lonely. He'd just spent the past few years trying hard to not think about his loss. He'd accepted some holes were too deep, too jagged to ever be filled. Keeping busy, head down, one day at a time. Now he found he was looking forward to seeing her, talking to her, watching her laugh. He shook his head.

"What are you thinking about, Joshua?"

He glanced at her. In the slight glow from the headlights, she was staring at him.

"Nothing."

"I was thinking about trying to explain what happened to the sheriff with all the holes in my memory."

He almost slammed on the brakes. "Really? I mean, um, yes, that will be awkward."

"There's no way I can make any headway unless you're there. You can tell him about my accident and all the things we found at my aunt's place."

"Those are facts, physical clues. The empty cabin, the vehicles in the outbuildings, your burned-out car. You just have to convince them to take a look, okay?"

She bit her lip.

"Tell you what. Let's work this out in the morning. I'm sure you could use a good night's sleep. It'll give that head of yours more time to heal."

She nodded. "Good idea."

He relaxed for a moment. Once he said he couldn't go with her to back up her story, she'd distrust him, wonder if he was some kind of fugitive. Actually that had been the plan he'd worked out with Fish and Game, but now he regretted it. He didn't want her to fear or hate him. He wanted her to…

Go ahead. Think it.

And that, too, was a problem. He'd finally stopped obsessively thinking about his family, his loss. She'd be leaving soon, and he'd need to concentrate all of his energies on his job. Not on her smile. Her wit. Her—

No. He clenched his jaw and stared at the road in front of him.

They soon pulled up in front of his cabin. He unhitched the trailer and put Horse in the barn, then went inside. "Are you hungry? I can fix us something to eat."

"No, I mean, maybe something for Izzy."

"I don't have any dog food, but I can make her a peanut butter sandwich, maybe add some cat food sprinkled over the top."

"Cat food? You have a cat? What's the kitty's name?"

"Cat."

"I should have figured it out." She glanced around the room.

"Cat's feral. I just put some food outside for her."

Her smile lit up her face. "Of course it would be feral. I really couldn't picture you cuddling up with a Persian named Mr. Whiskerfluff."

He found he liked her smile. Too much.

"Okay, I have to ask," she said. "You mentioned a cow."

"Yes, a Normande, a French breed. Name's Bo."

"Beau? What a lovely—"

"Short for Bovine."

She laughed. As he'd hoped she would. "I'd guess if you had a son, you'd name him Boy."

"David. I named him David." He touched the dog tags hanging around his neck.

Her eyes widened and blood drained from her face. "Oh. I'm so, so sorry," she whispered. "I had no—"

"'S okay, Bethany." He tucked the tags into his shirt. "It was a long time ago. Back to that cat food."

She was still pale, but cleared her throat. "Yes. Um. In a pinch I guess we can give it to Izzy. Cat food isn't designed for dogs. It causes all kinds of problems you don't want to know about. Oh, and just watch it when you offer it to her. See her big mouth and those tiny eyes?"

He nodded.

"No depth perception. You could lose half your fingers."

"Thanks for the warning." He quickly made Izzy her doggie sandwich. As warned, Izzy snatched it from him in a move worthy of *Jaws* and scarfed it down in three bites.

"Thank you," Bethany said.

He strolled to a closet and pulled out a sleeping bag. "Okay, bathroom's through there." He pointed. "Washer and dryer behind that door if you want to launder your clothes." He found a neatly folded long-sleeved T-shirt and placed it on the bed, then turned toward the door.

"Wait." She stared at the sleeping bag. "Where are you going?"

"I'm going to crash in the barn tonight with my critters. They'll love the company."

"But—"

"Staying in here just wouldn't be proper, ma'am."

A slight blush warmed her cheeks.

He stepped outside before he could say anything more. A cool breeze had swept much of the smoke away and a million stars gleamed above. The Psalmist's words came to mind. "When I consider the heavens, the work of Thy fingers, the moon and the stars which Thou hast ordained, what is man that Thou art mindful of him, or the son of man that Thou hast visited him?"

For the first time in a very long time, his mind wasn't filled with echoes of the past. It was just silence, and he felt at peace. The weight he'd carried for so long, all the what-ifs, had lifted and he could draw a deep breath without it crushing his ribs.

He pulled out the dog tags and kissed each one before returning them to under his shirt. His wife had ordered them as a Christmas present with their names etched on them. They were always close to his heart.

He reached the barn and threw his sleeping bag into the loose hay.

A diesel engine echoed in the distance, growing louder.

Joshua's chest tightened. *Who'd be driving around this time of night out here?* He rushed to the door of the barn.

Headlights appeared, pinning him in the beam before illuminating the space between the house and barn. He watched as a large black truck parked in front of him.

No time to get his shotgun, neatly stored next to the door in the house.

The driver turned off the engine, leaving the headlights on, and rolled down the window.

Joshua stepped toward the truck. "Can I help you?"

"Maybe." The voice was deep and harsh. "We're looking for a woman who may have gotten lost."

The hairs on Joshua's neck tingled. "And you are…?"

"Friends." The man stepped from the truck. A second man got out the other side and moved toward his cabin.

Sweat dampened Joshua's back, quickly chilling him in the cool night.

The passenger had reached his cabin and was briefly outlined when he opened the door.

Joshua clenched his fists. *Please, Lord, don't let them find Bethany.* He raised his voice, hoping Bethany could hear him. "What was she driving? Or was she on foot?"

"That's the thing. We're not sure." The man was backlit so Joshua couldn't see his face. "Mind if I take a look in your barn?" The question was punctuated by the sound of him racking the slide of a pistol.

The crunch of approaching footsteps on gravel unlocked Bethany's frozen legs. She'd seen the black truck approach and despite the fog in her brain, she'd recognized the vehicle. Now the passenger was heading to the cabin.

She started to scream, clapped her hand over her mouth and frantically looked around the room. She could easily see under the bed and the bathroom was tiny. Several doors were on the far side of the room. Joshua had pointed to one and said the washer and dryer were in there. That left the other door. *Please, dear Lord, let it be a back door.*

Her breath came in ragged sobs. She searched the room again. Her hiking boots sat next to Joshua's huge cowboy boots.

She snatched them, ran across the room and reached for the knob to the back door. She paused momentarily. But there was no time to put on her boots.

She started to turn the knob. *Wait.* If she opened the door, anyone outside would see the light. But if she turned it off, the faint glow around the windows would cease and they'd know someone was in the house.

Her hands were so sweaty she could barely grasp the doorknob. If she threw the door open and ran fast… *Who am I kidding? I can't run through the woods in socks.*

She turned and tried the door to the laundry area. A washer and dryer, remarkably new-looking, sat side by side with a laundry basket full of towels on the floor beside the washer. With the hoses and dryer duct, both machines were away from the back wall. A small space but just enough.

The footsteps grew louder, closer.

"Izzy, come," she whispered. She tossed her boots under the towels, then pulled the laundry basket out. She tossed the towels casually over the back side of the basket.

Izzy ambled over and Bethany shoved her behind the washer, then followed, shutting the door just as she heard the front door open.

Izzy must have understood the situation. She lay behind the dryer, seemingly content to be near Bethany.

Chair legs scratched on the oak floors followed by crashing. More heavy footsteps crossed the room, she figured to the back door. A squeak and a slam as the door was violently opened.

Bethany used the noise to move the laundry basket back into place. She lay on her side in the tiny space, closed her eyes and silently prayed. She was small and slim, but she knew the bottom of her legs and feet were extended beyond the washer and were behind the basket. Hopefully the towels would conceal them.

The laundry door screeched open. Someone stood in the opening, his breath coming in harsh gasps.

Bethany held her breath, hoping her pounding heart couldn't be heard. She put a reassuring hand on Izzy's leg, praying the dog wouldn't make a sound.

The door remained open, but the footsteps retreated. More banging around, a door slammed.

She remained motionless, frozen in fear. How many men were there? What were they looking for?

She already knew the answer. They were looking for her.

She tried to think, to work out what had happened to make her a target. It was all a blank.

A door opened and closed.

She tensed. Had he returned to the back door? If he looked in the laundry room she feared this time he'd find her. She was afraid to close her eyes, but more afraid to keep them open.

A tiny whimper threatened to come out of her mouth. Somehow she stifled it.

More slammed doors, the diesel engine revved, then grew faint before silence engulfed the house.

The dust behind the washing machine tickled her nose. She tried to swallow, but no saliva remained in her mouth. Her head pounded with her heartbeat, each thump a blow of pain.

"Bethany?" Joshua called her name.

She hadn't heard him come in.

"Bethany? It's safe. Where are you?"

It's a trap. They're making him draw me out.

The back door opened. "Bethany?" he called out the door. "They're gone."

Izzy whined.

"Shh." She patted the dog's leg and felt her tail thump.

The light went on in the laundry room. "Bethany?"

She turned her head.

Joshua's face peered at her, his eyes wide. "How on earth…"

The laundry basket beside her legs moved. His arm reached for her and she lifted her hand to grab it. He effortlessly pulled her sideways to her feet as Izzy scrambled out from behind the machines.

Her legs had turned to cooked spaghetti. She grabbed him to keep from collapsing and he half carried, half dragged her to a chair at the kitchen table.

"I…you…what…never mind." He stared at her. "I'm going to make some coffee. Or would you rather have tea?"

"I don't know. Either, I guess."

He stared at her a moment, reached over and plucked something from her hair, then showed her a dust bunny. "Friend of yours?"

"As long as it isn't a spider," she said without thinking.

"Another gem of memory. You don't like spiders." He turned to the coffeepot and filled it at the tap. Once the coffee was brewing, he pulled up across from her at the table. "Hiding like that. That was…you're very clever."

Heat rushed up her neck. His praise felt like a soft, warm blanket.

He leaned forward. "But I have to know—did you recognize either man?"

"I didn't see any faces, only the black truck. It was the same one that drove me off the road." She was surprised her voice sounded so calm. She was twitchy all over.

"They were looking for you."

She mutely nodded.

Izzy sidled next to her and leaned against her leg. She scratched the dog's neck.

"And you have no idea, no memory of why they'd be after you?"

She looked up at Joshua. His dark eyebrows were drawn over his eyes; his lips had thinned.

I don't want him angry at me. "I'm sorry," she whispered. "Everything's still a blank."

"Whoever they are, they seemed determined to find you." He stood and paced. "So…your sister and aunt are missing. You're driven off the road and left for dead. What could they want?" He stopped pacing and stared at her. "Before they drove off, they said they'd be keeping an eye on me, so they are suspicious that you're nearby."

"They must have found my car and discovered…" She clenched her fist. *Discovered there wasn't a body inside.* "Shouldn't we call for—"

"I already checked. Landline's still dead. And we can't just jump in the truck and head to town. There's only that one road. For all we know they're watching it."

"What are we going to do? We can't— Wait. No. Not *we.* They're not looking for you, but you might get in their way and get hurt—"

"Stop there, Bethany. I'm not about to throw you to the wolves to save my own skin." He gave her an intense gaze. "Not now," he muttered.

His words made her eyes blur and she glanced down at Izzy until she could blink them clear. She didn't know why, but she somehow felt it had been a long time since someone had cared for her safety. She liked the feeling.

Joshua saw the tears before she ducked her head and fussed over the dog. He rubbed his chin, moved to the counter and poured two cups of fresh coffee, glanced at her, then added cream and sugar to one cup. He placed the mug in front of her with a napkin, set the second cup across the table, then moved to a built-in set of shelves.

"Thank you." She took a sip. "Perfect. How did you know?"

"I suspect for now, we're both learning what you like." He slipped his hand down the side of the shelves.

Click! The shelves swung open.

"Oh!" Bethany slopped coffee on her hand. She quickly used the napkin to wipe up.

He caught the shelving unit before she could see what was behind it, reached inside and grabbed a white mailing tube, then shut the door.

"That would have been a handy hiding place," she said dryly.

"You wouldn't have fit. Although… I wouldn't have believed you'd squeeze behind a washing machine." He crossed to the table, opened the tube and pulled out a set of rolled papers. They proved to be maps. He flipped through until he found the one he was looking for and used the salt and pepper shakers to hold down two corners. He held the third corner while his coffee cup anchored the fourth.

The map was topographical, showing roads, elevations and streams. He pointed to a tiny black square. "This is us." His finger traced the driveway that dead-ended at his home. It joined a slightly larger road, all funneling down to a single county road. "All they have to do is wait here to see who's coming in or out. Or, if their primary interest is in us, they'd wait here." He pointed to another location.

"Where's my aunt's place?"

He leaned closer, aware of her sitting next to him. He briefly touched the dog tags at his neck before pointing out the location. "Here. And this is where your car went off the road. The fire moved up this mountain." He took a half step away. No matter what feelings were stirring, he didn't know if she was single. *She* didn't even know.

"What we need to do is cross a ridge to the next gulch that has a road, but it won't be easy as it'll be cross-country—"

"I can do it."

"I suspect you can. But that's only part of the problem. Yes, we'd avoid running into those two…thugs, but we'd still be a huge distance from town and anyone who could help you." His brow furrowed. "Unless…"

"Yes?"

He rocked back on his heels, then gave a short shake of his head.

"What?"

"It'll never work. You're just not—"

"Smart enough? Big enough?" Two red spots appeared on her cheeks. "Brave enough? Tough enough? How do you know what I can do?"

"*You* don't even know what you're capable of!"

Izzy whined and pawed at Bethany.

"Maybe not, but I know I can't stay here hiding out like some frightened rabbit." She stood. "Tell me your plan and let me decide if I can do it."

Joshua's mouth had dropped at her outburst. He closed it and nodded. "Right. Okay. Do you remember if you can ride a horse and read a map and compass?"

"I guess we'll find out."

He glanced at his watch. "We can't do anything until it's light, but at daybreak we'll see if my plan will work. Get some sleep." He moved to the door and picked up the shotgun he kept handy for varmints after his chickens. "Lock the door after me." He strolled out into the night. He didn't need a flashlight. The moon had risen and cast a deep blue light over the landscape. He stopped and looked out over the mountains marching away in the distance. The peace he'd felt earlier had been replaced by a deep apprehension. Bethany was obviously in trouble, but his help had to be in the background. If even a whiff of his identity surfaced, his own life would be in danger. And if anyone thought they could use this connection between them, her life would be in further danger.

He thought it would be hard to fall asleep, but he felt like he'd barely closed his eyes when the first gray light of morning peeked through the cracks in the unpainted barn walls. His rooster announced the break of day at regular intervals as if Joshua wasn't aware of the time.

He stretched out in his sleeping bag in the fragrant hay, feeling the stiffness from his lumpy bed, and went over his plan. If it didn't work, he'd need to come up with something else, but his options were limited by the remote and rugged terrain.

He wasn't sure if Bethany would be up this early, so he took his time doing chores—making sure the chickens had plenty of water and food, then checking on Horse.

He kicked around a bit longer before walking to his front door and knocking.

Bethany answered. She'd obviously taken a shower and had braided her wet hair. Her clothes were recently washed and slightly wrinkled. "Good morning."

He grinned at her in spite of himself. She was even prettier without the smudges of soot on her fresh-scrubbed face. "Morning."

She opened the door so he could enter. The aroma of fresh coffee filled the air.

"Did you want me to make some breakfast?" She moved to the counter and poured him a cup.

"You can cook?"

"Apparently."

He took the mug. Something was in her expression, a stiffness he'd not seen before. He walked over to the shelves, then turned back to her. "So you looked."

She froze for a moment. "I don't know what you mean."

She was a terrible liar. Her face was flushed and she couldn't meet his gaze.

He nodded toward the shelving unit.

"Yes." She shot him a swift glance, then took a deep breath. "So do you have hidden cameras here?"

He kept a straight face. "Nothing so high-tech. See the bird's nest next to the books? If you open the hidden door, the nest shifts."

"I see. Why do you have so many guns? And you had some animal skins and traps. Are you…a criminal or hiding out from the law or something? Maybe trapping illegally?" Her voice had grown higher.

He wanted to tell her the truth, that he *was* the law, but he couldn't risk it. The cover story they'd created was that he had a shady past and was hiding out. For the past fourteen months he'd been working on breaking up and arresting poachers killing endangered animals. When he had to go to town for supplies, the locals gave him a wide birth and warned their children to stay away from the man with the scar. He couldn't risk blowing open his investigation. "Let's just say I have a lot of enemies."

"Oh." She turned back to the small counter and made a production of wiping down the already spotless surface.

He sat down and relaxed his grip on the mug. "Bethany… um…were you able to remember more about your life?"

"A few fragments." She finally turned around. "I remember a farmhouse and looking out over a field. The smell of freshly cut hay. The sound of rain on a metal roof. I remember being alone. Not much to go on."

"It's something." He gave her an encouraging smile.

She nodded. "You mentioned a plan last night to get help."

"Right. We should have a bite to eat before we get started. It'll be a long day." And then she'd be gone, back to a world that didn't include him. He hadn't expected to care. But somehow, he did. He was finding out what he'd been missing. *Shake it off, Joshua.* He touched the tags, stood and moved toward the stove.

"I've got this. Scrambled eggs?"

He nodded.

She pulled a bin with several dozen eggs from the fridge. "You have either a lot of chickens or prolific layers."

"Both." He sat back down. "Assuming those two goons are

guarding the road here—" He pointed at the map still spread out on the surface. "We need to get past them and reach the sheriff. My horse trailer's already hitched up. I figured I'll just casually drive past them with the empty trailer. Even if they stop me, there's nothing to find."

She paused in stirring a bowl of eggs. "And I'm…?"

"Another couple of assumptions. *If* you can ride a horse and *if* you can read a map and compass, you'll be riding around them and meeting me here." He tracked her path on the map, his finger stopping where the gulch ended at the county road. "We'll load up Horse and drive to the sheriff."

"There's no one around here with a cell phone or landline we could call from?"

He shook his head. "In this area, everyone pretty much lives off the grid. Gravity-fed water systems, wood-burning stoves, lanterns. Some, like me, have generators. But my phone will stay out until I report it and they get around to sending someone out."

She turned back to the stove and dumped the eggs into a frypan. "Sounds straightforward. What about Izzy?"

"She'll be with me."

"Will they remember they didn't see a dog last night?"

"No reason to. The dog could have been in the barn or an outbuilding."

"I think this could work. So, what could go wrong?"

He glanced out the window. "Nothing. Unless one of those off-grid mountain men see you and decide you might be a threat."

She stopped frying the eggs and turned to look at him. "What would they do?"

"You don't want to know."

THREE

Bethany tried to push down her uneasy feelings about Joshua's gun stash, but his comment about the rogue mountain men wiped away whatever appetite she'd had. She served Joshua, dumped her eggs into a bowl for Izzy, then sat and nibbled on some dry toast.

"What about this farmhouse you remembered? Do you think you lived there?" He made quick work of breakfast.

"Maybe. I felt…comfortable. And I also remember the word 'hall.'"

"Like a hallway? Or a name?"

"I don't know. Maybe a hall in the farmhouse. It's all so frustrating."

He finished, stood and rinsed off his dishes. "Let's get going before those men decide to come back here for another look." He grabbed a fleece jacket, then led the way to the barn with Bethany and Izzy trailing behind. Once there, he grabbed a bridle, blanket and saddle, then opened the gate to the pasture where Horse was grazing. Horse nickered and approached. Joshua reached in his pocket, took out a treat and handed it to Bethany.

She looked at it, then at him. "What do I—"

"Don't think about it. Let's see if muscle memory will take over."

She nodded and held out her hand with the treat.

Horse didn't hesitate. He grabbed the crunchy round horse candy from her palm.

Joshua held out the bridle and Bethany took it, then immediately slipped the reins around the horse's neck. With her right hand, she grabbed the bridle's crown, reached between the horse's ears and held it. Her left hand expertly slid the bit into the horse's mouth. A quick buckle of the throatlatch and Horse was bridled. "Well, I guess I do know about this." She smoothed the forelock over the browband, then stroked Horse's soft muzzle. It all felt natural.

He handed her the saddle blanket.

She tossed it into place, smoothed it out, then reached for the saddle.

"It's heavy."

She nodded, took the saddle, then flipped the fender and stirrups over the seat. After turning her back to the horse, she swung it easily onto Horse's back. The saddle had both a front and back cinch and she navigated placing both, then stood back and stared at her work. "How strange to have no memory of riding or horses in general and yet…" She shook her head.

He handed her the map and a compass, then tied a bit of rope around Izzy's collar to keep her from following Bethany. "Head southeast following the creek as much as possible." He pointed. "Horse is sure-footed and fast, so trust him." He tied the fleece jacket behind the cantle and adjusted the stirrups.

She quickly mounted and turned Horse toward the trail.

"Bethany—"

She glanced back at him.

"Be careful."

She stared at him, an unreadable expression on her face. "You, too." She clicked at Horse and he set off at a slow canter. She had no doubt that horses had featured prominently in her life. The rocking lope felt as natural as walking.

Horse slowed as the trail grew steeper, picking his way down the mountainside. Joshua and the cabin disappeared and the forest embraced them, the only sounds breaking the stillness being the steady clatter of hooves against the dirt in a syncopated rhythm.

They came to a cliff. The rushing of a stream below told

her they'd arrived at the creek Joshua had referred to. At first she didn't see a way down. She dismounted and explored the sharp drop for a few moments. She finally located the game trail, overgrown with bracken fern. She patted Horse. "I know Joshua said you were sure-footed, but I think we'll both walk at this point."

She started down, sliding at times, making sure she stayed well ahead of Horse. She didn't want the thousand-pound animal to land on top of her.

When they reached the stream, she remounted and turned Horse downstream.

Boom!

She jumped and looked around for whoever was shooting.

Boom, boom!

Were they shooting at her? Had the two men from last night found her? Her breath came in gasps. She urged the horse to go faster.

A man stepped in front of her, blocking the trail. He had a black, unkempt beard, greasy hair under a ragged and oil-soaked baseball cap, and a filthy flannel jacket. He'd pointed his rifle directly at her midsection. "Just where do you think you're goin', girly-girl?"

Bethany's mouth dried. She grew lightheaded. She couldn't seem to form words.

Something clattered behind her.

She turned in the saddle.

Two more men, equally as rough and unkempt, were behind her on the trail. Both were mounted on mules. One smiled, exposing yellow-stained teeth. "Well, lookie here, fellers. We got ourselves someone we need to take to our brother."

The man in front moved toward her and reached for the reins.

Bethany let out a shriek, whipped the reins out of reach, and kicked Horse into a gallop, knocking the man aside. She leaned over the horse's shoulder, making herself as small as possible should they start shooting.

Her eyes blurred from the cool wind. Passing tree limbs raked her back. She couldn't hear sounds of pursuit over the thunder of the horse's hooves.

She lifted up to see the path…just in time for a sapling that had fallen across the trail to smack her across the shoulders.

She flew off Horse, landing with a jarring thud.

The world grayed, then blinked out.

Joshua watched until Bethany was out of sight, then bowed his head. "Keep her safe, Lord," he whispered.

Izzy seemed content to follow him to the truck and get a helpful boost to the passenger side. He got in and headed down the driveway. He'd deliberately left his rifle and sidearm at home. If the men stopped him and found him armed, it could escalate the situation. He needed to be as unthreatening as possible.

The day was clear and sunny, with only a hint of the smoke from yesterday's fire lingering in the air. The tamaracks were just starting to turn yellow as the season changed. This would normally be the kind of fall day to relish and enjoy. Now he had to make an effort to keep from grasping the steering wheel with a white-knuckled grip.

As he'd expected, the black diesel pickup stretched across the dirt road. The same two men from the night before stepped out as he approached. He rolled down his window. *Be calm*. "Morning. Looks like you haven't located your friend."

"What? Oh yeah, that." The larger of the two men scratched his unshaved chin. "Don't worry. We have reason to believe she didn't get far."

While they were speaking, the second man strolled to the rear of his horse trailer and was inspecting it. He slowly circled around the back, then moved forward on the far side, looking into his truck bed. He ended up on the passenger side where he inspected the cab.

Izzy growled.

Joshua's heart thumped faster. He patted her side.

"What kind of ugly farm dog is that?" the man next to him asked.

"Bull Terrier. Excellent rat dog." *And good at identifying one when she sees it.* He made an effort to keep his face neutral.

"Where ya headed?" the man asked.

Joshua gritted his teeth. He wanted to whip out a badge and demand to know who they were and why they were so interested in Bethany, but he had to keep undercover at all costs. Even the local sheriff didn't know who he was, which was why he was so successful. "Picking up a new pack horse. And I'm late, so if you don't mind…"

The two men looked at each other and the bigger man shrugged. "Sure. We'll check back with you when you return."

"You do that."

The smaller man pulled their black truck forward and Joshua glanced at the license plate. 1A followed by seven numbers. 1A was Ada County. Boise. As soon as he was out of sight, he jotted the numbers down on a scrap of paper. His success in working undercover meant that he could have no observable connection to the law enforcement agencies. When he'd finished an investigation or had something to report, he'd drop into the post office and send a post card to "Uncle Roy." The postmaster, an elderly, retired firefighter, would hand him a package containing a special satellite phone. He'd make sure no one had followed him and would place the call, give his report and return the package to the post office. His caution kept him safe from discovery. The postmaster believed Joshua was a reclusive millionaire, loved the intrigue, and kept the phone charged.

Even the hidden closet was a carefully thought out trap. The men he was investigating were very cautious and clever.

He knew they'd searched his cabin at least twice. It was only a matter of time before they discovered his hidden cache of guns, ammunition and endangered-species pelts. Once they found this, he expected them to eliminate the competition—try to kill him—or pull him in. Either way, he'd nail them.

Three months ago, he'd been notified that there was a mole at the department. Until they found out who was leaking information, he was on his own.

It was an extremely dangerous life he lived. His one avenue of escape was his safe house in Orofino should he need it. He'd inherited it from his maternal grandparents and it was still in their name. The people he was dealing with had a propensity for murdering anyone they had even an inkling of suspicion was connected to law enforcement.

He told no one his true identity. Unfortunately, that meant that Bethany would have to trust him while thinking he was some kind of fugitive or shady character.

He reached the meeting site, parked the truck and trailer, then brought Izzy out for a walk. The chunky dog cheerfully wandered around the grassy field next to the road and trotted back to him, tail wagging, when he called. He put her back into the truck with the windows down.

He checked his watch. If Bethany kept up the quick pace, she should be arriving soon.

A half hour later, the staccato clatter of hooves shattered the silence.

He'd been leaning against the truck. He straightened, his heartbeat increasing as he thought about Bethany. He couldn't help the grin that spread across his face. But it faded almost as quickly. She hadn't given any sign she saw him as anything more than a safe harbor in a storm. Temporary.

Horse burst from the trees. Riderless.

Joshua became rooted to the spot, unable to breathe.

Horse spotted him, slowed, then walked over.

He automatically reached in his pocket and handed the horse a treat. The move shook him out of his frozen shock. He ran his hands over his horse, pausing at the saddle. The jacket was still tied to the back, but pine needles had been caught up in the saddle strings. More needles poked into the saddle blanket.

She'd obviously been knocked off. The question was how badly was she hurt? And could he find her?

Bethany's eyes flew open, her lungs straining to get air. She stared up at the cerulean blue sky lined by treetops. She was on her back... *Why?* In a rush the memory crowded into her brain. Horse. The tree that had flung her off. Her hitting the ground and getting the wind knocked out of her.

The men after her.

This last thought propelled her upward. *Get moving.*

She stood, still trying to draw a deep breath. Everything ached, but thank the Lord, nothing was broken. Her head reminded her of her earlier accident and she longed for aspirin. She glanced down the trail. As expected, Horse was gone. She was on foot. The men were mounted and would soon catch up with her. *Think. Think!*

They were mountain men, used to tracking game and living off the land. They'd take one look at the tree across the road and the disturbance in the dirt and know she'd been knocked to the ground. To her left, thick cedars and pines pressed against the trail. The tumbling stream was on her right.

She turned left and walked four steps into the trees, making sure her footprints showed in the dirt and grasses. Her stomach churned and mind whirled with the pressure of wanting to run, to get as far away as possible. When she reached the thick carpet of pine needles, she reversed, stepping backward, making sure only one set of prints leading away would appear. When she reached her starting point, she crouched, then jumped into the stream.

Frigid water poured into her boots and swirled around her knees. The current pushed her downstream, her steps slipping over the glassy-smooth, polished rocks. She knew she was making a lot of noise, but she had to make as much progress as possible before the men caught up.

She reached a point where a large pine had landed in the stream sometime in the past. The rotting trunk now created a small waterfall with a deep pool on the other side. Mossy rocks edged the creek.

She stopped and listened. She wasn't certain if the thumping she heard was her own heart or the clatter of the mules' hooves.

A large, flat boulder lay over an undercut bank and was relatively free of moss. She carefully clambered out of the rushing water, crawling on all fours to make sure she left no footprints on the rock.

She continued to crawl.

"Do ya see there?" One of the mountain men's voices carried clearly to her.

Adrenaline shot through her. She dropped to her stomach. Her body felt rooted to the rock. She had to push herself to slide sideways until she'd reached a thick, drooping cedar branch. *Please, dear Lord, please help me.*

Murmuring voices, words indistinct, went on forever—or so it seemed.

Her nails dug into the pine-covered ground. She squeezed her eyes shut.

Then…nothing.

Had they moved on? Followed her false trail? Split up?

Or were they waiting for her to move, thinking they'd gone?

She counted to ten, then fifteen, before opening her eyes and lifting her head to see if she could spot them. She could see no evidence of them through the fragrant, fernlike boughs. *I can't stay here forever.* They'd soon realize they'd missed her and retrace her possible movements.

She stood and assessed her surroundings. She would have to figure out how to get past the deep pool if she stayed with the stream. Moving away meant climbing the hillside behind her while making sure she left no footprints. And going as fast as possible.

No time to ponder. She started up the mountain.

Her boots were soaked, and squeaked with every step. As she was already cold from the creek, the cool fall afternoon chilled her further. She concentrated on putting one foot in front of the other, seeking the hardest ground.

Overhead a chipmunk chattered his disapproval at her passing.

She paused, catching her breath while looking around for any sign of pursuit.

Boom! Boom!

The unmistakable sound of gunfire echoed somewhere in the distance.

She jumped and moved faster up the mountain. *I can't outrun a bullet.*

Leaving the water-loving cedars behind, she soon was moving between ponderosas, their trunks larger and wider-spaced. If those mountain men were nearby, they might spot her in the open areas between the pines.

Minutes later, she came to a large wall of rocks rising steeply in front and beside her. She couldn't navigate them without climbing gear. She paused behind a craggy trunk and peered around to get her bearings.

As she walked, she'd continued southwest toward the rendezvous site. Far below, the stream had narrowed and reached an area where the water had carved a constricted passage. No one could maneuver that direction. If any of the men had investigated that route, they'd know she hadn't gone that way.

Maybe they'd moved on.

Almost as soon as she had that thought, something flashed from the opposite mountain.

She ducked behind the tree and assessed her choices. She could climb straight up, keeping the tree between herself and the men on the opposite mountain, but all they had to do was move sideways and they'd see her. She flipped through her options at lightning speed.

She could stay put, wait until dark and then move, but she had no way to see where she was going. And it would be colder then, and the jacket Joshua had given her was still on Horse.

She could assume they hadn't seen her and make a run for it.

She could pray and hope Joshua found her.

"Dear Heavenly Father. I'm in a terrible mess and need Your divine guidance."

After her prayer, no flash of insight or divine inspiration came to her. She leaned against the trunk, then slid to a sitting position and wrapped her arms around her knees.

She was alone, probably lost, with three men after her and two more possibly waiting for her. All of them seemed bent on hurting or killing her.

She rested her head on her knees.

In a flash, pictures poured into her brain. She remembered.

Joshua had made sure Horse was uninjured, running his hands over each leg and checking the hooves. He'd started to mount up, but paused. Izzy. It wasn't safe to leave her in the truck. Even though it was cool and the windows were open slightly, the sun would shift. There would be no shade in an hour or two. Bethany said the dog was hardly a tracker, but she might be useful. At any rate, he didn't want to leave her. After making sure he had any medical supplies Bethany might need, he returned to the truck and opened the door.

The chunky dog got out, stood next to him and wagged her tail.

"You ready to find your owner?"

She let out an enthusiastic bark.

He didn't trust that her short legs and stocky build would be able to keep up. He lifted her and tucked her forty-five-pound body under one arm, then mounted Horse. Once in the saddle, Izzy squirmed until she'd wrapped around the pommel, then relaxed. Her front legs poked straight out as if she were Superman soaring through the sky.

He turned Horse toward the trail and set off at a lope. He didn't want to dwell on what-ifs, but they pushed into his conscience. What if Bethany were severely injured in the fall? She was still recovering from the car accident and fire. This fall could easily have reinjured her brain, making it more difficult for her to recover her memory. What if the Messick brothers had stumbled upon her?

He stiffened at that last thought. The brothers were bad news everywhere they went. They were known poachers, but small fry, not taking the endangered species but primarily hunting deer and elk out of season. If he were still working regular Fish and Game duties like he'd done when first hired straight out of college, he would have arrested them by now. When his undercover work ended, they'd be on his radar.

Don't forget the missing women.

Sweat dampened his shirt. Five missing women over the past eight years. They could be involved in that.

Then there were the two men staging the roadblock. He didn't know how they fit in with all that was going on with Bethany.

About three miles from where he'd parked, he found the downed tree across the trail. He dismounted, holding Izzy still in the saddle, and studied the ground.

Horse's shod footprints were clear, heading down the trail below the fallen tree. Bethany's fall showed in the disturbed earth under the tree. Next to that were the footprints of at least two mules, based on the narrower shape. The mules were unshod. *The Messick brothers.*

A finger of dread snaked up his spine. He refused to let the dark thoughts take over. *She's okay.* She *had* to be okay.

The mule tracks had gone up the hillside across from the stream.

Izzy whined and wiggled to get down. "Bethany assured me you weren't a tracker," he whispered. "Let's prove her wrong." He lifted the dog from the saddle.

She trotted over to the stream and began to drink.

"Looks like she was right." He mounted Horse. "Come on, Izzy, find Bethany."

Instead of following, Izzy waded into the rushing water.

"Izzy, come!"

She ignored him and continued downstream.

His stomach clenched. He needed to find Bethany before… He shook his head. He shouldn't have put the dog down.

I could just leave her—

He dismissed the thought as soon as it popped into his head. The poor dog wouldn't last more than a few hours before the coyotes or a cougar found her. He turned his horse into the creek, crossed it, then tracked the dog up the hillside.

Izzy waded downstream until she reached a waterfall above a small but deep pool. She climbed out of the creek bed and ambled toward, then past him, breaking into a run.

"Dog, you're asking for a heap of trouble—"

Bethany stepped out from behind a tree.

The dog launched herself into the woman, almost knocking her over with her enthusiastic greeting. "Oh, smart Izzy! You weren't fooled for a minute." When Izzy's tongue-swiping, tail-thumping greeting slowed, Bethany looked up at him. "Do you think I can thumb a ride with you?" She grinned.

Joshua grinned back, dismounted and walked toward her. "Sure. But what about—"

The thump of hooves and tumbling rocks came from behind them.

He turned.

The Messick brothers appeared and stopped, though their rank body odor drifted around them like an odoriferous fog.

Joshua moved Horse so Bethany was on the other side, then turned to face them, casually letting his hand slide inside his jacket. “Aren’t you three a bit far from home?”

“Just checkin’ out the landscape,” Otis, the oldest brother, said. “Thought our youngest brother might find her interesting.”

Though every muscle in Joshua body had tightened, he stared them down. He wasn’t armed and there were three of them.

Otis’s gaze drifted toward Joshua’s hidden hand. He scratched his chin, then spit on the ground. After what seemed like hours, he jerked his head toward his brothers.

The three of them turned their mules and headed back down to the trail.

Bethany came around the horse and watched them leave. “Did you show them a gun or something?” She rubbed her arms. “I got the feeling they don’t give up easily.”

“They don’t. And I don’t like that.” He scratched his cheek. “You ran into them earlier?”

“How do you think I ended up on the ground? We were hightailing it down the trail.”

“Smart move.” He glanced at the mountain rising above them.

She saw his gaze. “Thought I could get away by following the stream on this side, after sending them in the wrong direction, but I got cornered. My only option was to retrace my steps.”

“You were going to risk running into them again? Out here, in the wilderness?” His voice had risen.

“I wasn’t going to be cornered like a wild animal. And that rather painful fall managed to rattle my brain. Some of my memory returned.”

"You obviously didn't remember you were unarmed."

"Not quite." She raised one arm. Her shoelaces dangled from her fingers, attached by a patch of fabric. Stepping away from Horse, she swung the laces in her hand, then let go of one side. A rock flew out and cracked into a tree. "I remembered I knew how to make a David's sling." She began untying the shoelaces. "I remembered why I came out here in the first place. And I remember I was almost murdered because of it."

FOUR

Bethany didn't look at Joshua until she'd re-laced her boots. When she did, she couldn't read his expression.

"Ready?" he asked. "Are you going to tell me what you remembered?"

"Yes." She started past him down the mountain, not waiting to see if he followed.

"Excuse me..." Joshua was right behind her. "But exactly *when* are you going to enlighten me?"

"Soon. I just want to be away from the Messick brothers."

"Your nose should give you a thirty-minute warning."

She grinned in spite of herself. "So true, so true."

Izzy cheerfully trotted ahead, found a stick and carried it high in the air like a drum majorette at the head of a parade. They reached the downed tree and passed under it.

"Wait," Joshua said.

She paused and looked back at him.

"No use wasting a perfectly good horse." He swung up into the saddle and stuck out his hand.

She tried to keep the relief off her face. Her head pounded, a whole new bunch of muscles she didn't know she had were aching, and her feet hurt from the drying boots. She grabbed his outstretched hand.

He lifted her as if she weighed nothing and swung her behind the cantle. His fleece jacket, still tied, padded the stiff leather of the saddle. She didn't mean to, but her head swam from his lifting her up, so she grabbed him around his waist. His warmth reminded her of how cool the day had become. She didn't let go.

Soon they arrived at his parked pickup and trailer. She didn't wait to be lifted down, quickly sliding off Horse. Her memory may have been returning, but she still had no idea of who he was and why he had a hidden area of his house with maps and guns.

He followed suit, though he shot her a questioning glance. Silently he loosened Horse's cinch, replaced his bridle with a halter and loaded the gelding into the trailer.

"Are you going to tell the sheriff about those three men?"

Her question came as he shut the trailer behind his horse. "The Messick brothers? Did they hurt you?"

"I think they wanted to."

He gave a short jerk of his head. "No doubt. But we need to concentrate on your missing sister and aunt. I'll drop you off—"

"You're coming into the sheriff's department with me, right?"

He looked away. "I have to find a place to park my rig. You need to go on in and file a report. I'll catch up with you."

Her doubts about him surged again, but she simply nodded, waved Izzy to the truck and lifted her inside, then joined her. The washboard dirt and gravel road gave way to a paved surface. Pine trees pressed in on both sides of the road, blocking the surrounding mountains. They passed occasional logging trucks, ATVs and pickups.

Joshua eventually broke the silence. "I have admirable patience, but it's run out. Back to your memory. You said you remembered more."

She toyed with Izzy's ears for a moment, her mind weighing how much to share. She finally took a deep breath. "My name is Bethany Hall. I live a few hours south of Coeur d'Alene. I'm a freelance presentation designer specializing in graphic design."

"What is that?"

"When someone needs illustrations for a presentation—sort of a visual storyteller."

Joshua gave her an encouraging smile. "Go on."

"Now it's your turn."

His eyebrows rose. "My turn?"

"You can't know about me and I know virtually nothing about you."

He touched his chest, then fiddled with the steering wheel. "Okay. Fair deal. Joshua McGregor. Thirty-two. Single. Your turn."

She opened her mouth to protest his lack of information, then sighed. She really wanted to know more about what had happened to his son, how he got his scar, what he was doing in the middle of nowhere with a hidden cache of maps and guns, and what the story of those dog tags was, but apparently she'd have to pry every detail from him.

"I'm twenty-six. Si—" She was about to say single, but was she? Why did she have a scrap of memory of an engagement ring? And why did the words *Never again. Shattered trust doesn't mend* resonate in her mind? And what was with the smell of something earthy, sweet and tart?

"Um…are we almost there?"

"Almost." He cleared his throat. "Still your turn. Why are you here and why might you be killed because of it?"

"I was doing research on my family, made some phone calls and discovered I might have a relative in the area. My sister and I decided to visit. I think there was something about that visit… about the fact that no one knew my sister and I existed. Something that made us a liability… I don't know. It was clearer in my head after landing on the ground. Your turn."

"You want to know about the scar."

Warmth burned up her neck and onto her cheeks. She mutely nodded.

"The three of us, my wife, son and I, were flying to Boise for a conference. My wife had her pilot's license. The plane developed engine problems. We crashed."

His voice was low and gruff, barely loud enough to be heard over the sound of the truck.

She'd been watching him, but her vision blurred and a lump grew in her throat. The scar in his heart was far deeper and more jagged than the one on his face.

"After I lost my wife and son," he coughed, "I didn't want to live. Not really. I couldn't see the point of waking up every day. So I found the most dangerous, most remote job I could. Somewhere no one knew me. Somewhere I didn't have to feel anything except the cold and the risk. It was easier that way."

Neither spoke.

More vehicles filled the road as houses came into view. "When we get to the sheriff's department," he said, "go in and file that report."

"Did you want me to mention you?" She watched his expression closely.

He looked out the window. "No."

"Just asking. What then?"

"I'll find you."

Somehow, she doubted she'd ever see him again.

They drove through town, passing modest homes, gas stations, a grocery store and an elementary school, before he pulled into a parking lot. He pointed. "The sheriff's department is in that building."

She hesitated. "What about Izzy?"

"She can stay with me."

That somehow reassured Bethany. Joshua may be a fugitive from justice, but he wouldn't hurt her dog. She jumped from the truck and turned to wave, but he'd already driven off. She watched him for a moment, then trotted toward the two-story brick building.

Inside, she stepped up to a glassed-in desk manned by a uniformed officer. "What can I do for you?" he asked.

"I'd like to see the sheriff."

"Your name?"

"Bethany Hall."

"And why do you want to see the sheriff?"

"I think my sister and aunt were abducted."

The officer blinked, then walked out of sight. Soon, the door beside her swung open, revealing a man in a Western-cut jacket. A bolo tie with a pyrite stone glinted under the fluorescent lights as he stepped forward. "I'm Sheriff Williams. I understand you want to report an abduction."

"Yes." She suddenly felt woozy and reached for the counter next to her. Her headache, never far from her consciousness, thumped away.

"Are you okay?"

"Yes. I'm just…a lot has happened." She straightened.

He stared at her for a moment. "Okay. I'm going to let Deputy Green take your report." He stepped aside and a stocky officer appeared. "Right this way, Ms. Hall." Deputy Green motioned for her to follow him. He led her to a desk with a few files and a computer and waved her to the nearby chair.

Bethany sat.

"Let's start with the basics." He placed his hands on the keyboard. "You said your name was Bethany Hall. Address?"

She gave it.

"And your sister's full name?"

"Ruth Ann Hall." She rattled off Ruth's address, then the information on her aunt.

Deputy Green entered the information, then nodded at her to continue.

She relayed the events of the past two days.

After she'd finished, he hit Enter, then leaned back in his chair. "Well, now, that's quite the story. I—" He leaned forward and stared at the screen. "You said you were driving your car—"

"When I was run off the road. Yes."

"Do you have an Idaho driver's license?"

"Of course."

"And your car had an Idaho license tag?"

"Yes. But what does that have to do with—"

His eyes narrowed. "Ms. Hall, if that's what your name really is, there is no record of you in our data base. No driver's license, no tax records, nothing to indicate you ever lived in Idaho. Now, do you want to tell me who you really are and why you're here?"

Joshua pulled away as quickly as he could and turned on the first cross street. A black truck had been trailing them for miles—just far enough back to stay inconspicuous. But Joshua had noticed. He needed to change out his obvious truck and horse trailer and see who was behind them.

He drove a bit farther before pulling into a large parking lot and driving around to the back. He'd barely stepped from the truck when a young man appeared beside him. "Hey, Shawn. Is the doc in today?" Joshua asked him.

The veterinary technician nodded. "But he's slammed with work."

"That's fine. I'm not in a hurry. How about if I leave Horse here and you can get to him when the vet has time? His teeth need to be floated and do a fecal to see if he needs worming. I'm not sure when I'll be back to pick him up, so you may need to board him as well."

"No problem. There's an open stall over there." He pointed.

"Mind if I leave my truck and trailer here?"

"Nope. Just park by the side of the barn as usual, Mr. McGregor."

Though Joshua didn't like leaving the animal, he knew Horse would be well cared for. He'd known the vet for years and knew he'd be too busy to take care of the equine's routine work right away. After settling Horse in the roomy stall, he got Izzy out of the truck and once again tied a small rope around her collar. Izzy might have been fine in the mountains, but he had no idea if she'd go after a cat in town or sprint out into the road.

Checking carefully to be sure no one was about, he made his way on foot through the back streets until he reached his safe house—a small, green-painted cottage on a shady side street. He let himself in with the key he kept hidden on the back porch. The house smelled stuffy, but it was otherwise clean. He had a local lady come in once a week to make sure the house would be available to him should he need a place to duck into. He'd made sure they never met; he used an alias, paid in cash and had told her he was a mining consultant and traveled often.

The garage held his battered, black, older Jeep Wrangler. Izzy seemed content to settle in the back seat and flop on her side. With only a slight hesitation, the engine fired up. He backed out, closed the garage door, then pulled into the street. He turned toward the sheriff's department, eyes searching for the black truck that had followed him. Not seeing it, he circled the block, then parked in the shade where he could watch both the sheriff's office and the street.

Shortly, Bethany stumbled outside. Her face was pale and she seemed unaware of where she was.

He stepped from the Jeep and called her name.

She first walked, then ran toward him, eyes wide.

Had her injury gotten worse? If so, he'd need to take her to the hospital. She slammed into him and clung to him as if he were the only thing to keep her from falling. Her breath came in ragged gasps.

"What is it? Get in. I'll get you to the doctor—"

"No, no, it's not that." She got into the Jeep, then reached back to pet Izzy. The dog greeted her as if she'd been gone for weeks. "You know who I am, don't you, girl."

He slipped in beside her, not knowing what to expect.

She stopped petting the dog and looked at him. "Where's Horse? And your truck?" Her voice was shaky.

"Both safe. What happened?"

She took a deep breath and slowly let it out, obviously trying to calm herself. The effort didn't seem successful. "They can't find me in their computer. It's as if I don't exist." Her jaw tightened and her breathing turned shallow. "Do…do you think I may have made everything up? That my name isn't Bethany Hall? That what I think of as returning memory is… I don't know, maybe something I once read or saw on television?" Her voice wavered a bit at the end.

"I don't know. You recognized your aunt's place, and some strange things were going on there. I heard your car crash and pulled you from the fire—"

"My car! What did the license plate on my car say?"

"I didn't look. I was focused on getting you out."

"Oh." She frowned. "Maybe we could go back to the accident site and see if we can recover—"

"Your car is a burned-out shell. After I got you out, it was fully consumed. Let me drive you home. You're sure to have enough there—bills, receipts, your contact information, computer, your pre-accident life. The rest of your memory might return as well."

"That's a couple of hours' drive. Are you sure?"

He nodded. He started the engine, pulled forward and turned left after scanning the road for the black truck. "I think we were followed. To play it safe, I'm taking a detour. If I tell you to duck, don't wait. Understand?" He glanced at her.

"Yes. Who do you think it could be?"

He shook his head. He'd thought about making contact with his department and reporting all that was going on, but he still didn't know what that was, nor if the mole had been discovered. All he had were pieces. Two possibly missing women. A car accident. Two men hunting Bethany. And a woman who didn't exist, according to the police search. What did it all mean?

"I'm sure you'll be glad to get rid of me."

Bethany's comment interrupted his thoughts. His hands tightened around the wheel. He should want to be done with this mess, with her. And yet… He glanced at her, then back at the road. "No. I—" He clenched his jaw. How did you tell someone that your whole world had ended once, and you'd chosen a life so remote, so dangerous, because you didn't care if it ended again? And now, finally, he was starting to care.

The silence stretched between them. The tires hummed against the pavement, but his mind was years away—graveside. Burned photographs. Echoes of laughter that still haunted his sleep.

Something up ahead caught his attention. A black pickup.

"Duck!"

Bethany dove to the floor of the Jeep.

With one hand on the wheel, Joshua flipped open the glove box. His fingers closed around the camo hat. He yanked it low over his forehead, shoved on the sunglasses he'd grabbed from the visor, and kept driving.

The windows were down in the truck pulled off to the side of the road and he could easily see two men inside. He kept his attention on the road. Once he passed the truck, he watched the rearview mirror to see if they followed.

They remained parked.

He let out the breath he didn't realize he'd been holding. When they moved around the bend and he could no longer see them, he said, "All clear."

Bethany slipped back into her seat. "Same men?"

"Yes."

"Why me?"

"I don't know. Somewhere, locked in that faulty memory of yours, is the answer. And those men don't know that. They must believe you are a danger or threat. Which means, whenever your memory comes back, we have to be prepared."

Bethany replayed the interview with the deputy over and over in her mind, but no matter how she analyzed it, she kept returning to the same, impossible conclusion. Either she was delusional about her own identity, or someone had deliberately erased her existence. Both answers terrified her.

"Joshua, what would it take to delete information about me in the state database?"

"I was thinking the same thing. If someone scrubbed you from the system, we're talking high-level access. Government, corporate, maybe even black market tech. That kind of operation doesn't come cheap. Do you know anyone like that?"

"I don't think so."

"What about your sister or your aunt? They're the missing ones. You they tried to eliminate."

Her heart rhythm quickened and she grabbed the door handle. "But you saved me. And you believe I'm not crazy."

"No, not crazy. But you are more interesting than the average person."

She snorted. "As are you."

The two-lane road unfolded ahead, winding through small towns, golden fields with grazing cattle or sheep, and mist-covered mountains. Autumn had painted the smaller bushes, cottonwood and aspen trees a brilliant yellow. The sparse traffic proved to be logging trucks or men in camo with rifles mounted on their pickup's rear window. Elk hunting season had opened.

After they passed the tiny hamlet of Clarkia, she had him slow down, then pointed to a mailbox next to an almost invisible road. He turned on the dirt drive and carefully wove around potholes partly filled with water from a recent rain before breaking out into an open field.

Bethany's muscles tightened in her chest, making it hard to breathe. She wasn't bonkers. She immediately recognized her modest, 1940s' Craftsman-style home. In the pasture behind the house stood a weathered pole barn. She jumped out of the Jeep almost before Joshua had put it into Park. "I have a spare key under the flowerpot—" She jerked to a stop. All of the potted plants she had on the front steps were missing.

Joshua caught up with her. "What's wrong?"

Before Bethany could answer, a woman stepped through the front door. "Can I help you?" She had short gray hair and wore a red flannel shirt, jeans and duck boots.

"Who are you?" Bethany squeezed her hands into fists. "And what are you doing in my house?"

"*Your* house? Hardly. I've lived here for thirty-five years."

"That's impossible," Bethany whispered. Her fingers dug into her palms. "I—I can describe every inch of this house. The scratches on the back door from Izzy, the loose floorboard in the kitchen—"

"You need to leave," the woman cut in, voice hardening. "Now."

"Are you kidding me?" Bethany's voice rose. "I'm calling the sheriff. You've broken into my home and—"

The woman pivoted and stepped into the house, slamming and locking the door behind her.

"Joshua." She turned to look at him. "I don't believe this! What's happening? This is my home. I—"

Joshua grabbed her arm but stared toward the house. His jaw tightened.

She looked in the same direction.

The woman had returned to the porch, this time with a shotgun. She raised the rifle.

Bethany's heart thudded loudly in her ears. She blinked, hoping her eyes were deceiving her.

The woman remained, eyes now narrowed.

Joshua subtly moved in front of her, his body tense. "Ma'am, let's not escalate this." He pivoted Bethany around, whispered *Go,* then hustled her back to the Jeep.

"But—"

He started the engine. "We won't get anywhere with someone

aiming a shotgun at us." He stopped at the end of the driveway. "We need someone to verify your identity. Who would recognize you? A neighbor?"

"Ha. No near neighbors."

"Someone from your church like your pastor?"

"I watch church on television."

"The postmaster, someone at the grocery store?"

She shook her head.

"What about your work? Do you have a company you usually work for or a colleague who knows you?"

She stared bleakly ahead. How had she become this isolated? The only people who knew her were missing. "I know there must be someone, but that part of my memory hasn't returned."

Joshua turned left, heading back the way they'd driven. They rode in silence for a bit.

Bethany tried to concentrate on the memories she did have, but all she did was to reawaken her headache.

Joshua had slowed as they were passing through one of the small towns. He put on his blinker and pulled off the highway.

"What are you doing?"

"Two things. We need to grab something to eat. And I need to check something out."

She realized they'd turned into a roadside café. Instead of parking in front, he pulled around to the rear of the building and parked under some big trees. After letting Izzy out for a quick run, they locked the dog in the Jeep with the window down, and Bethany followed him into the café.

A waitress paused in pouring coffee to a patron. "Sit anywhere, hon."

Joshua moved to a table by the window and pulled out a chair for Bethany. Before she could ask him any questions, the waitress dropped off two menus and two glasses of water. After she moved away, Bethany asked, "Well?"

"I'm following up on a hunch. I think that woman was

planted in your house. She's now seen you, my Jeep and me. I'm guessing she made a phone call to whoever is funding this scheme as well as the two goons driving that black pickup. If my hunch is correct, those same two men are now on the move, looking for us. There are only so many roads around here."

Bethany picked up the glass of water. She was grateful her hand didn't shake. After she took a drink, she said, "I can't keep hiding."

"For now, that's about all you can do until we unravel this mystery."

The waitress came over and took their order, although Bethany didn't have much of an appetite. She knew Izzy would be delighted to eat any leftovers.

"Your memory… Let's try something." Joshua leaned forward. "You've recovered some, but are there any random thoughts you've had?"

"Like what?"

"Things that pop into your mind for no reason."

Bethany looked at her left hand. "Yes," she said quietly. "I found myself rubbing my ring finger and feeling as if I'd had an engagement ring there."

Joshua sat up straight. "Oh. Well, of course. A woman as beautiful as you is probably—"

"No, that's not it." She reached across the table and grabbed his arm, then immediately let go. Warmth spread up her neck and onto her cheeks. "With that memory came the words *Never again. Shattered trust doesn't mend.* And a smell. I think whoever I was engaged to is now engaged, or married, to my sister."

Before Joshua could respond, their meal arrived. They ate silently, though Bethany mostly picked at her food. When the waitress brought the check, she also brought a doggy bag. Bethany shoveled her burger inside.

Joshua finally spoke. "Bethany…what if you weren't just erased? What if you're the reason your sister is missing?"

FIVE

Bethany tried to sort through her racing thoughts. *How dare he accuse me of hurting my sister and aunt? What if he's right? Either way he doesn't trust me.*

Angry, she got up and stormed out of the café and drew in a ragged breath. She should take Izzy—

Rapid footsteps came up behind her. Joshua coming to question her some more?

Before she could turn around, arms grabbed her from behind and lifted her off her feet. The carton of food for Izzy flew from her hands.

She tried to suck in enough air to scream, but a calloused hand covered her mouth. She clawed at her attacker's hand and kicked backward. *If I can just twist out of his grip and get back to the café—*

"Stop struggling or we'll kill your dog," the man whispered harshly in her ear. His breath smelled of stale cigarettes.

She froze.

Whoever held her spun her around toward the parked Jeep. A second man had reached through the window and was stroking Izzy with one hand. He held a pistol aimed at her head with the other.

Her stomach dropped. Sweat dampened her back and her legs grew weak.

"Do you understand me?" the man whispered again.

She nodded.

"I'm going to take my hand away from your mouth and you're going to get into the back of our truck and I'm going to tie you up. If you try to run, scream or fight me in any way, the dog dies."

Bethany couldn't answer around the lump in her throat. She nodded again.

He released his hold around her, grabbed her arm and dragged her toward the end of the parking lot, where a black truck with a double cab was parked. After he opened the doors, he spun her around and quickly zip-tied her arms behind her back. He hoisted her into the back seat, slammed the door and got in. He started the engine and pulled forward.

Bethany couldn't take her eyes off the man with the gun pointed at Izzy.

He stopped petting the dog and dashed for the truck, jumping into the moving vehicle.

She lurched toward the door.

The passenger turned around and pointed the pistol at her. "I can shoot you just as easily as I could shoot your dog."

Her vision narrowed on the barrel of the gun pointed directly at her head. "You won't get away with this." Her mouth was dry as the Sahara. "You'll—"

The man laughed. "You don't get it, do you? No one will be looking for you. You don't exist."

"Joshua—"

"Will be taken care of just as soon as we finish with you."

The driver jammed the accelerator, almost hitting two young boys on bikes as they charged out of the parking lot. She made sure one of the boys saw her and mouthed, "Help."

"Settle down, lady." The gunman reached for her.

She shrank back into her seat. *Okay, okay. Think. You can't outrun a bullet, but you can outsmart these two henchmen.* "Who wants me erased?"

"None of your business."

"Are you willing to do the dirty work for this person? Go to prison—"

He waved the gun at her. "You need to shut your yap before I really get mad."

She looked around. They were heading north. Maybe she could get someone's attention. If they had to stop for gas, she could make her move.

They slowed, then turned off the highway.

She gasped as she recognized the road.

They were going to her home.

The gray-haired woman she'd seen earlier met them as they drove up and parked. As soon as the passenger door opened and she saw Bethany, her face tightened. "You fools!" She practically spit the words at the man with the gun. "Tony, what were you thinking? You—"

"Don't rile me, woman!" The man she called Tony shoved the woman aside, opened the back door and hauled Bethany from the truck. "Orders directly from the boss." He shoved Bethany toward the house. "You did get the place cleaned out?"

"Almost." The three of them followed Bethany up the stairs and into the living room.

Bethany came to an abrupt halt. She was in a dream. A nightmare. Her memory of the room slammed into her brain, followed immediately by the reality in front of her. The room had been stripped of all of her personal items—photographs of her and her sister, her original art, hand-thrown pottery, the quilt she'd purchased at the last craft show—all gone.

She didn't have time to absorb the changes. A shove from behind sent her flying forward toward her art studio in the back of the house. As she passed, she glanced up the steep narrow stairs leading to her bedroom on the second floor. The handmade rug at the top of the stairs was missing.

She had the same overlapping memory and reality when she saw her studio. She knew what *should* have been present and the void of the present. All the art was gone, though her easel, taboret and drafting table remained.

A violent shove sent her to the floor, cracking her knees painfully on the hardwood floor as she tried to keep from landing on her face.

Tony shoved her to her side, pulled out a zip tie and grabbed her leg.

She pulled her other leg back to kick him.

"Do it and I'll hurt you so bad you'll want to die." The hate in his gray eyes made her blood turn to ice.

She stilled and he tied her legs.

"Now, what's left to get out of here?" Tony asked the woman.

"There are still some boxes upstairs, and the last of..." The voice dimmed as she walked out of the room with the two men. The door shut with a firm bang, followed by the click of the lock.

Joshua glanced at his watch. The café felt louder now, the clatter of silverware and hum of conversation grating against his nerves. He spotted a dark truck up the street, driving slowly. If the two men were notified of their showing up at Bethany's house, they should be coming through any time now. He strolled to the door for a better look.

Wrong pickup.

Too much time had passed.

And Bethany was alone. Outside.

He jerked to his feet, threw some bills on the table for a tip and headed out the door. He'd taken one step into the parking lot when he spotted it.

The contents of the doggy bag strewn across the ground.

Joshua's pulse kicked into high gear as his eyes searched the lot. There was no sign of Bethany. He scanned the ground. Just beyond the food, the dirt lot was scuffed, the marks erratic, interrupted by deep tire tracks. Truck-sized tracks.

A jolt of dread went through him. His eyes darted over the lot, searching for more signs of a struggle. There was no immediate sign of violence. No blood. But the tire marks weren't promising.

The tire tracks seemed to come from the south—the alley running behind the row of businesses—and head north. That would make sense as the men were last seen south of here.

But where did they go? And how eager were they to kill Bethany? It was one thing to slam their big pickup into a car and send it off the road, quite another to murder someone face-to-face.

"Lord," he whispered. "Send me guidance."

Izzy barked.

He raced to the Jeep and opened the door.

The chunky dog jumped down, trotted left and sniffed the air, then made a beeline to the burger. Before he could stop her, she wolfed down the food.

"Come on, Izzy." He patted the passenger seat.

Izzy scampered over and allowed him to boost her up. He slammed the Jeep into gear and started to tear out of the parking lot when he spotted two boys walking their bikes down the sidewalk. He pulled up and rolled down his window. "Excuse me."

The boys warily moved a few steps away.

"Did you see a black truck come out of this lot a few minutes ago?"

"I'll say," the taller of the boys said. "Almost hit us."

"Which way did they turn?"

Both boys pointed north.

"Thanks." North toward Bethany's home. It was nearby and remote. And that strange woman claiming to live there had to be part of all this. He'd start looking for Bethany there.

He drove as fast as he dared. He should call in law enforcement, but by the time someone would show up, it could be too late. Every second counted. He found himself clutching the dog tags as he prayed to find her.

It seemed to take forever to reach the mailbox marking the

driveway. He drove past, trying to get a glimpse of the house. The trees were too dense.

Keep going? Check it out? Direct frontal approach? But if she weren't there, he'd have wasted time looking for her here.

But her house was a perfect location to take her. Bethany said she had no neighbors. And the old woman claiming to live there was just *wrong.* He knew that with every fiber of his being.

A hundred yards down was an old logging road. He patted Izzy, made sure the Jeep was in the shade and well hidden, partially rolled down the windows, then set off through the woods toward Bethany's house. He moved as silently as he could through the underbrush, pausing every so often to listen.

He'd reached the edge of the yard when he saw it.

Parked in the front of the house was the black pickup.

After they locked her into her studio, Bethany wasted no time. She pushed herself across the floor to her taboret. *Please, please, dear Lord, let them not have emptied the rolling set of drawers.*

She grabbed the drawer pull with her teeth and tugged. Slowly, too slowly, it opened.

Yes! The drawer still held all her assorted drawing supplies, including her craft knife.

Thumping overhead told her they were emptying out her bedroom. They'd soon return. She had little time.

Turning her back to the drawer, she reached inside with her bound hands. Her captor had pulled the zip ties so tight her hands were going numb, yet she rummaged around, feeling each shape for the metal handle of the knife.

Thump, thump, thump.

They were coming downstairs. At any moment they could check on her.

A cold rivulet of sweat trickled down her back. Her fingers

skimmed the items frantically…and then she found the craft knife.

One set of footsteps clumped toward the studio.

She swiftly tucked the knife into her sleeve, shoved the drawer shut and rolled away from the taboret.

The door clicked open and the woman stepped into the room. She stared at Bethany for a moment. "You should have died in that car crash." She turned and left.

Bethany clenched her teeth to keep them from chattering at the hatred in the woman's words. The second the lock clicked, she flipped the knife around and sawed at the zip tie. It seemed to take forever; her partially numb fingers kept slipping on the smooth metal.

Finally she managed to cut her hands free. Then her legs. She stood, and rushed to the window. She was facing the pasture and barn. How far could she reasonably run? And what if they spotted her before she got out of sight? She couldn't outrun a bullet.

What did she know, remember about this house, this room? *Quickly, quickly. Think.* The studio was…new. Added on. *Yes.* When she had this room added, the closet enclosed the space under the stairs and continued across the wall for lots of storage space. A small crawl space was left under the bottom steps, hidden by a piece of wallboard.

She opened the window, then raced to the closet on the opposite wall and removed the wallboard.

Footsteps approached.

She swiftly crawled into the cramped space.

The lock clicked open.

She pulled the wallboard back into place and held her breath.

One of the men let out a yell. Two sets of thumping footsteps followed.

"You idiot—"

"I thought you tied her—"

"You should have shot her—"

"Get her back!"

The shouted argument abruptly ended and from the sound of footsteps at least two of them left the room.

Bethany tried to breathe as quietly as possible.

Rustling, then thumping. Someone was tapping on the walls. As soon as they reached the panel she was behind, they'd know it was hollow. She shifted, slowly inching around.

Thump! Thump! Thump! The sounds drew closer.

She rotated until her back pressed against the panel and her legs were braced against the wall.

Thump!

The blow reverberated against her back and rattled her teeth. She squeezed her eyes shut. *Please, please, please.*

The hammering against the walls continued, now moving away.

Something dropped into her hair and skittered across her head.

She clapped her hand against her mouth to keep the scream from escaping. She wanted to jump up and slap at her head and clothing. Instead she remained still as the spider crawled to her shoulder.

A distant shout sent the person still in the studio clattering out of the room.

Bethany wasted no time. She moved the wallboard and shot from her hiding place. She took a moment to whack at her clothing and hair, then charged away from the calling voices to the front of the house. They'd go back and find the wallboard had been shifted, but hopefully she'd be long gone.

Joshua slid closer to the house until he could both see and hear what was going on.

Loud male voices and the slamming of a car door interrupted the silence.

He froze for a moment.

More yelling and slamming doors.

His breath hitched.

One of the men ran from the house, slamming the door behind him, then raced around back.

Joshua ducked, then peered through the foliage.

The woman who'd earlier confronted them with a shotgun left the house. She disappeared around the corner, appearing shortly driving a large white van.

Joshua tried to read the license plate, but he was at the wrong angle.

"Do you see her?" a man's voice called from behind the house.

Joshua exhaled sharply. Bethany must have escaped.

"Not yet." The second man's voice came from the pasture.

One of the men ran around the house and called to the woman, "Go ahead and leave. We'll stay here and get her, then put her in the house and burn it as planned. Meet up at the arranged place." As the white van drove off, Joshua shifted until he could see both men working their way toward the barn. *Oh Lord, don't let them find her.*

A flicker of movement at a window caught Joshua's attention. He turned to see Bethany slip through the front door. She paused, looked around, then bolted toward the highway.

He looked around, found a couple of ponderosa pinecones, then chucked the first one in front of her.

She slowed.

He threw the second cone. This time she looked in his direction. She shifted course and was now running towards him.

He moved a branch so she could see him more clearly. She flew into his arms. He wanted to hold her and keep on holding her.

He glanced at the men in the distance.

They had turned and were running straight toward them.

“Let’s go.” He seized her hand and raced toward the Jeep. This time he didn’t worry about noise.

The sound of gunfire rang behind them. One of the men was blindly shooting at them.

They ran faster, plowing through the tree branches trying to snag them, jumping over fallen logs.

Bang!

Bark from a tree trunk in front of him flew in the air.

His lungs seized, his legs felt leaden, his pulse raced. His hand, still gripping Bethany’s, was slippery with sweat. Still, he raced on.

He spotted his Jeep just as a bullet hit the door. He thought he heard Izzy yelp.

Crouching low, he approached the vehicle from the other side. He pushed Bethany into the back seat, leaped into the front, started the engine and floored the gas. He didn’t slow down when he reached the highway and prayed no one was driving by.

“Joshua.” Bethany’s voice was strained. “Izzy’s hurt.”

“How bad?” He didn’t take his eyes off the road.

“It looks like the bullet scraped her neck. There’s…a lot of blood.”

“Okay. Hang on.” He pushed the Jeep harder, wishing for a more powerful vehicle. “How’d you escape?” he finally asked.

“I know my home far better than they did. I needed to buy time and create a false trail, so I left the window open and hid. As soon as I heard the outside doors slam, I made a run for it.”

They’d reached a junction in the road. “Bethany, I can drive north to see if we can find the nearest veterinary hospital, but that will put us on the White Pine Scenic Byway with few road options should the men catch up with us.”

“What else can we do?”

“Head west on Highway 6 toward Potlatch. A lot more roads, but Izzy would have to wait a bit longer for help.” He looked at her through the rearview mirror.

"Those men will kill me, kill us, if they find us. Go west."

He sped up. He could drive around them if he took State Highway 9, or loop around—

"Joshua."

He looked at her through the rearview mirror.

Her brows were furrowed and her expression grave. "What's beyond Potlatch?"

"We'll run into Highway 95. Go north and we'd come to Coeur d'Alene. South is Moscow—"

"And Pullman, Washington," she finished for him. "Washington State University."

He nodded.

"When I say that, I have a feeling of tremendous sadness. An empty hollow. Something bad happened there."

He remained silent. Another piece of her memory might be dropping into place, but he longed to reach out and give her a comforting touch.

"Do you think if we go there, I'll remember?"

"It's worth a try. Somehow we need to figure out why these people are after you." He drove as fast as he could over the winding, two-lane road, passing through rolling hills covered in pine, small farms and simple homes. He constantly checked for any sign of pursuit. They had a white van as well as the truck, so it was possible they could split up and cover two directions. He prayed they'd stay together and take the northern route.

He finally relaxed his grip on the wheel slightly when they reached the tiny hamlet of Potlatch where several roads converged, opening up more possibilities to escape. They finally arrived in Moscow, home of the University of Idaho and a scant eight miles from Pullman. He began looking for a vet hospital and soon spotted one. He parked on the side, got out and opened the rear door, then froze.

Bethany cradled the injured dog in her arms. Blood was smeared across her cheek and the front of her shirt. She'd used her jacket to stanch the bleeding from the dog's neck. Izzy was motionless, eyes closed.

He reached for the dog.

She wrapped her jacket around Izzy's body as he lifted her out, then stepped out herself. There was blood on her pants, too. She looked like she'd just survived a war.

As they entered the vet hospital, heads turned.

A woman in overalls holding a border collie shook her head. "Gunshot, huh? Guess we need to start painting our pets fluorescent orange so these hunters see 'em."

Joshua didn't reply. Instead he shadowed the receptionist as she quickly ushered them into an exam room smelling of disinfectant and wet dog. The vet, a middle-aged woman wearing half glasses and hair pulled into a loose bun at her neck, bustled in. While her nimble fingers slid over the dog, she peppered them with questions. "How did this happen?"

"Um, hunter," Bethany answered. "Definitely a hunter."

"How old is she?"

"Four. Shots current." Bethany held on to the exam table with a white-knuckled grip as the doctor completed her assessment. "Will...will she be okay?"

"She has lost a lot of blood, but she's in good health and the wound is fresh. We'll stitch her up, but I'd like to keep her overnight, just to be sure."

Bethany looked at Joshua. He gave her a slight nod.

"Okay."

"I'll need you to give the front desk all your information, including a phone number." For the first time the vet looked up from the dog and at them. "I'll take care of...what's her name?"

"Izzy."

"I'll take care of Izzy."

"We'll have to call you," Joshua said. "We don't have a phone." He gently propelled Bethany into the lobby where a technician handed him the registration form placed on a clipboard. He had Bethany sit and handed her the pen. She stared at the blank form for a bit before starting to write.

He scanned the room, then stood.

They needed to keep moving. Fast.

As soon as she'd finished writing, he grabbed the clipboard and returned it to the front desk, then ushered Bethany to the Jeep. He got into the driver's seat, then glanced over at Bethany.

She was sightlessly staring forward.

"Look, Bethany, I know you're upset about Izzy. We don't have to go into Pullman just yet—"

"No. I *have* to go there. Someone tried to kill me, wipe out my existence, move into my house, steal all my possessions, kidnap my sister and aunt, and shoot my dog. I need to find out who, and why." She looked at him, her expression fierce. "I need to get my life back."

Bethany closed her eyes for a moment, marshaling her thoughts. Izzy was in good hands. She needed to focus on the elusive memory connected to Pullman. No. Not just Pullman. Washington State University. Did she go to school there? She shook her head slightly. That didn't seem right. She opened her eyes and glanced at Joshua. He stared at her with an unreadable look. "Drive toward the university, please," she said.

He put the Jeep into gear, checked for traffic, pulled out and turned left. He didn't speak as they headed toward the town, as if instinctively knowing she needed to be alone with her thoughts.

Bethany tried to identify her feelings. Loss. Hurt. Emptiness.

Fear.

A chill swept through her. Did she even want to know the answer to what was happening? She looked at the blood caked on her shirt. Izzy's blood. Her eyes filled with fresh tears, but she wiped them away and gritted her teeth. Somehow, she had to find out what was happening.

She nearly gasped as Joshua suddenly swerved into a Walmart parking lot. “What are you doing?”

He parked some distance from any other vehicles. “We have to be careful. Not memorable. Stay under the radar. Right now you look like someone out of a horror movie.” He opened his door. “Stay here. I’ll be right back.”

Before she could say anything else, he’d left.

She slid down in her seat and tried to make her mind a blank. After a few minutes, scenes flashed through her head. A parade, people in plaid shirts, the scent of popcorn. An old, unpainted wooden building. Her sister grinning at her, sunlight striking her hair. Floating in an inner tube down a cold river on a hot day. An outdoor café rich with the aroma of freshly brewed coffee. A single word, *pierce*.

A few raindrops tapped on the windshield. She hadn’t noticed before, but dark clouds had gathered, blocking the late afternoon sun. The rain increased slightly before settling on a steady rhythm. Lights came on around the parking lot and it seemed as if the temperature drastically dropped. She’d left her jacket wrapped around Izzy and she shivered in the damp coolness.

She finally spotted Joshua running toward the Jeep, hands full of plastic bags. She opened the back door for him. He threw in the bags, then ran around and jumped in.

She nearly hugged him after he shut the door. It startled her, the strength of it. He’d helped her, protected her, believed in her when no one else would. *But this isn’t love.* It couldn’t be. It was gratitude tangled with adrenaline and confusion. Nothing real could grow in a storm like this…could it?

The words—*Never again. Shattered trust doesn’t mend*—swarmed into her mind.

“I spotted the rain and went back for a jacket for you.” He studied her face. “Have you remembered more?”

"A jumble of images. A river, café, a festival with a parade, and the word *pierce*."

"A name?"

"I don't know."

The rain increased, now drumming on the roof, making them seem cocooned and isolated, even though they were surrounded by parked cars and trucks. She shivered again.

Joshua turned on the engine and cranked up the heat. "This rain doesn't look like it's gonna stop anytime soon, and in a couple hours it'll be dark. I think we need to stay here tonight. We don't know where those men are. They may decide to wait for us to return to my place. And besides, this way we'll be here to pick up Izzy tomorrow."

"Sleep in the Jeep?"

He smiled.

She liked his smile. It was like sunshine pouring through clouds on a dreary, overcast day. What was she thinking? Had she forgotten that she knew next to nothing about Joshua? How quickly she forgot he could be a fugitive.

"No. We'll find a motel. Get a couple of rooms. You can clean up, we'll grab some dinner, and go over the fragments of your memory."

It seemed so strange to have someone making decisions, but she felt too drained to come up with a different plan. Clearly she'd lived on her own for some time.

They drove back into Moscow and found a motel. "I'm going to check in, get us unloaded, then find someplace to hide the Jeep."

"I thought you said they'd go back to your place."

"Educated guess, but we don't know what these guys will do or how extensive this group is. They may call in reinforcements."

Bethany wrapped her arms around herself. "You're right," she said softly.

Joshua soon returned with two sets of key cards. He drove the Jeep around to the back of the motel, parked and grabbed the bags out of the back seat. "Wait here until I get your door unlocked." After opening one ground floor room, he tossed several bags inside, then waved her to come in.

She jumped out and raced through the rain to her room.

"I'm going to take care of the Jeep." He shut the door. "Lock it."

She did so, then crossed the nondescript but clean room to the bathroom. Her face in the mirror made her gasp.

She did indeed look like someone out of a horror movie, with rain-smeared blood dripping off her chin. She quickly rinsed her face and hands, then picked up the Walmart bags and checked the contents. Besides a spiral-bound notebook and travel-sized toiletry kit, she pulled out an oatmeal-colored sweater, white T-shirt, denim jacket and jeans. Everything seemed to be about the right size.

She showered, dressed and left her bloodstained shirt and pants soaking in the sink.

By the time she'd dried her hair Joshua still hadn't returned. Maybe that had been his plan all along—first chance he got, he'd leave her someplace.

She raced to the window and peered between the drapes. The rain had settled into a steady shower and dusk had fallen. The parking lot in front of her was about half-full. Beyond was an alley with a line of trash cans against the back fences of the adjacent homes.

She stepped to the small desk and checked in the drawer. As she'd hoped, a pen with the motel's name and logo was inside. She sat and wrote the scraps of memory she'd had. Parade. People in plaid shirts. Not just plaid. Flannel shirts. Popcorn. Old, unpainted wooden building. Floating in an inner tube down a cold river on a hot day. Outdoor café smelling of coffee. Pierce. She slammed down the pen in frustration.

Someone softly tapped on the door.

She jumped, then stood and peeked out the window.

Joshua stood at the door, dripping wet, holding a pizza box and plastic bag.

She quickly opened the door and fought the urge to hug him, gave up, and embraced him, rainwater and all.

"If you'd like, I can leave and return again."

She laughed.

"I brought dinner. Cold by now, but still food." He whisked past her and placed the box on the desk, then picked up her notebook. "I see you've been busy while I was gone. Hopefully, the key is written here. We can only play hide-and-seek for so long. And they're very determined."

The pizza wasn't totally cold and they were both so hungry that it didn't matter. Bethany sat cross-legged on the bed while he sat in the frayed blue chair by the window. Whether it was the spatter of rain on the parking lot asphalt or the sight of Bethany in the oversize sweater on the bed, he felt relaxed for the first time in days. He wiped his fingers and mouth on the provided napkins, then leaned over and picked up her jotted notes. "Could use a computer about now."

"That's what I was thinking. Did you see a computer in the lobby when you checked in?"

"No. We can check some of this out tomorrow at the library. Are any of these memories connected?"

"The first couple of things, the shirts, parade and popcorn—seem to be."

"Plaid, maybe flannel, shirts mean not a summer parade. I know Orofino has Lumberjack Days in the fall—"

Bethany jumped off the bed. "Yes, yes, that makes perfect sense. My aunt sold jam or jelly at different festivals I…" She rubbed her forehead, then looked at the ceiling.

He silently waited while she struggled for the memory.

"My sister, Ruth, and I and…anyway, about a year ago, we went to that festival. We'd been tracing our family history and… discovered we had an Aunt Nan."

"Your parents didn't tell you?"

"They died when we were very young. Car accident. We were taken in by a wonderful couple…anyway…" She began pacing. "We met Aunt Nan. I remember she had a booth at the festival and she invited us to come and visit."

"Why didn't she reach out to you after your parents died?"

"Because…because she… I don't…" She ran her hand through her hair and paced faster.

She looked so overwhelmed that he stood and put his hands on her shoulders to slow her agitated movement.

She froze, eyes wide, staring up at him.

A warmth bloomed in his chest—unexpected, undeniable. For a moment, the rest of the world faded. The feel of her beneath his hands, the look in her eyes—it was like something fragile and fierce had cracked inside him. He caught his breath, startled by the sudden, sharp pull toward her.

It wasn't just sympathy anymore.

It wasn't just protecting her.

He let go, abruptly, almost as if he'd touched a live wire. "Sorry," he muttered, stepping back too fast.

She didn't move right away. "'S okay," she said softly, her voice barely audible beneath the sudden swell of rain against the roof.

"Pier—" Bethany cleared her throat and began again, louder. "Pierce. It's not a name, it's a place. Ruth and I took a trip to Pierce, Idaho, to check out a lead on our family's background. We went to the historical center there."

"We should pay it a visit." Joshua scratched his day's growth of beard. "Can you remember anything more on what happened at WSU?"

"No. Just a feeling that it wasn't good."

"We'll check it out tomorrow." He stood and moved to the door. "Bethany—"

"Yes?"

"Um…lock the door behind me." He left before he could make a fool of himself. This was ridiculous. But even as he walked away, the lie clung to him like his wet clothes. Return to his life?

What life?

Dealing with people who slaughtered rare animals for their skins? Long stretches of silence? He'd carved out something bearable in the isolation, sure—but not *meaningful*. Not *alive*. Bethany had changed that.

At first, it had been about protecting her. A responsibility. But somewhere along the line, it became more. She challenged him, leaned on him, trusted him. And now, her pain felt personal. Her fight, his fight.

He told himself he was staying to see justice done, to untangle the mess someone had made of her life. But the truth was simpler—and harder to admit. He wasn't ready to let her go.

He unlocked and entered his room, then leaned against the door. He had to get his thoughts off Bethany and back on the mystery surrounding her. Back on the clues they needed to follow up on. It was easier, and safer, to concentrate on that. It kept him from thinking about his tangled feelings toward her.

When he lost his family, he'd decided God wanted him to remain single. The scar on his face made that an easy choice. Women always turned away when they saw him. But Bethany didn't flinch when looking at him.

Maybe that was pity.

He shook his head violently to shake the thought away. Instead, a different thought shoved its way in. He hadn't reached for his dog tags. They'd acted like a shield, a touchstone up until now, a reminder of where his heart was buried—with his high school sweetheart, the only girl he'd ever dated, the only one he'd ever loved.

Until now?

Enough.

Tomorrow, he told himself, they'd find answers. For tonight, he just needed to sleep and stop thinking about a certain woman with reddish-brown hair.

He tossed and turned all night, finally catching a few hours of sleep just before dawn. After getting dressed, he peeked out the drapes and checked the weather. No rain. And Bethany was just about to knock on his door. He opened it and tried to hide the grin. "Morning."

"Oh. Good morning. I wasn't sure if you'd be up."

"We have a lot to do today. Any new memories?"

"Not new. I wrote out my sister's and aunt's full names and addresses, listed the events in order. And sketched the faces of the two men and the woman." She held up the spiral pad.

He opened it. The drawings were done in pen and were very accurate. "That's right. You did say you did things like this. Like a graphic designer, right? Clearly you can also draw. You could be a police artist."

Two red spots appeared on her cheeks. "Before we get started today, do you think we can pick up Izzy first?"

"Of course. We'll grab something at a drive-through on the way." He picked up the Walmart bag that held the few items he'd bought for himself. "Wait here while I get the Jeep..."

"I'd rather come with you. I need the exercise."

He nodded and started walking toward the alley where he'd stowed the vehicle.

"Joshua?" She easily kept pace with him.

"Yes."

"This is awkward...um...about Izzy. I... I don't have any

money to pay her bill. If I could get a loan, I promise I'll pay you back."

"You don't—"

"I do. I owe you my life, Izzy's life and so much more."

"Bethany." He stopped and she almost ran into him. "We can deal with that later. I'm a firm believer that you shouldn't worry about tomorrow. Every day has enough by itself. Okay?"

"Matthew 6:34."

"Your memory is coming back quite well, I see."

"I just need to remember why those people want me dead. And why my sister and aunt are missing."

They found the Jeep unharmed, grabbed some coffee and scones, then liberated Izzy from the vet hospital. The dog had a shaved neck on the one side and an impressive line of sutures but seemed quite thrilled to see both of them.

Once everyone was loaded up, Joshua turned to Bethany. "Check out the WSU campus?"

"I think so. Something may be familiar. Then the library."

Before taking off, Joshua took the small black pouch he'd bought at the store. It was designed as a jogging belt. He placed his wallet, a small Swiss Army knife and a book of matches inside, then pulled it on. He had no idea what they'd encounter, and a handgun would be extremely handy, but he could hardly buy one at Walmart.

They drove the scant eight miles separating Moscow, Idaho, and Pullman, Washington. The rolling hills of the Palouse surrounded them, fields tan with wheat stubble. The air was rain-rinsed and cool, the sky a clear blue, and the traffic was light.

Bethany straightened when they reached the edge of Pullman. The sprawling campus was perched on several hills. Joshua was about to turn toward the university when Bethany grabbed his arm. "There. Do you see that café over there?"

He signaled a turn and pulled into a small parking lot next to the outdoor seating.

"I know this place. I've been here before. With…with Daniel."

"Who's Daniel?"

The light was suddenly gone from her eyes. "I don't know."

SIX

Bethany didn't want to get out of the passenger seat, but the only way she'd ever wake up from the nightmare she was in was to get answers.

Several dog bowls filled with water and a customer at a table with a golden retriever on a leash showed this to be a dog-friendly café—as did the name, The Sit and Stay Café.

Bethany picked up Izzy's leash and stepped out of the Jeep. Izzy beelined for a table at the far right, found a spot under the table and sat. The aroma of freshly brewed coffee and fresh bread surrounded them. "Looks like Izzy knows this place, too," Bethany said to Joshua as they both took seats.

A waitress soon approached and handed them menus. "What can I getcha?"

"Coffee to start for me." Bethany looked directly at the waitress. "Do you know me?"

The young woman blinked. "Should I? Are you, like, famous?"

"I don't think so. I was just wondering if I'd been here before."

"No idea. I just, like, started two weeks ago." She gave a nervous grin. "I'll bring ya your coffees." She headed inside where she walked over to an older woman. After they spoke a minute the older woman glanced at Bethany a few times, nodded, picked up a coffeepot and two mugs, and brought them to the table. She poured the coffee, then set the pot down. "Is there something maybe I can help you with?"

"Have I been here before?" Bethany asked.

The older woman frowned. "You don't know?"

"She was in an accident," Joshua said. "We're trying to work on her memory."

The older woman narrowed her eyes and studied Bethany's face. "Well, a lot of people come and go—" She spotted the bull terrier. "Izzy!" She got on her knees and petted the tail-wagging dog. "What happened to her neck?"

"Long story." Goose bumps erupted on Bethany's arms. "So you remember Izzy?"

"I may not be good with names and faces, but I never forget dogs. Whatcha doin', girl?"

Izzy had flopped onto her back and was enjoying the belly rub.

"When was I last here?" Bethany gripped the edge of the table.

The woman paused for a moment and rocked back on her heels. "Oh, let's see. It has to be at least a year, maybe more. You were usually with that good-looking fellow." Her glance drifted to Joshua. "No offense."

"None taken." Joshua leaned forward. "What can you tell us about the man that was with Bethany?"

"Not much more than what I just said." Her brow wrinkled for a moment. "Allison used to work here around that time. She lived to gossip and knew everything about everyone. Maybe she could help."

Bethany caught her breath. "How could we get hold of Allison?"

"Give me a minute." The woman took out her cell and began to scroll, finally stopped and touched the screen. She put the phone to her ear. "Yeah, hi, it's me. Hey, remember the bull terrier, Izzy…yeah…um…right. The gal that owns her is here and wants to ask you a question or two." She handed Bethany the cell.

"Hi, Allison. To make a long story short, do you remember the man I used to come here with?"

"Of course. You should, too."

A snippet of memory sidled in. People smiling and clapping. "I don't."

"Come on. It was a big deal."

Bethany clutched her coffee mug, feeling the warmth. "Sorry..."

"You got engaged to him right there at The Sit and Stay." She continued to talk, but her words had no meaning. Bethany's head buzzed, and darkness lapped around her mind.

Joshua took the cell from her limp hand. "Hi. I'm sorry. Bethany...um...isn't feeling well. Could you tell me what you know about Bethany and..."

"Dan? Sure. But Bethany—"

"Like I said, she isn't feeling well."

"Okay, so, Bethany and Dan—that's Daniel Adams—got engaged at the coffee shop. It was so fun and goofy and we were all in on it."

"When was this?"

"Let's see, about a year and a half ago I'd say. Spring semester."

Bethany tried to focus on the end of the conversation she could hear.

"And who is Dan?"

"Dr. Adams. He's a professor at WSU. Business or economics, something like that."

"Thanks so much. We'll look him up—"

"I don't think he's still teaching. Maybe took a long sabbatical or something."

"Thank you so much for the information, Allison. We'll be in touch." He disconnected while she was still talking and handed the cell back to the waitress. "Thanks. Do you remember Dr. Daniel Adams?"

"Sorry. No." Something caught the woman's attention. "I gotta get back to work. Is there anything else?"

"No, thanks. You've been great."

It took Bethany a moment to notice Joshua had slid his chair closer, his hand gently enveloping hers. A quiet warmth spread through her, her pulse quickening at the tenderness in his touch—a flicker of longing she hadn't felt in years. But then the words surfaced, sharp and unyielding: *Never again. Shattered trust doesn't mend.* With them came the scent of something earthy, sweet and tart, twisting the warmth into a familiar ache of betrayal.

She straightened and casually withdrew from his gentle grip. "I'm fine." She answered his unspoken question. "I'm guessing the words that keep going through my head refer to a broken engagement. When we were at Aunt Nan's place, I had a memory about an engagement ring and the thought that my sister was now engaged to the same man. It came and went so quickly that I almost forgot about it." She looked into Joshua's quiet gaze and her breath caught for a second. "I…um…we should look up Daniel and see if he can fill in some blanks. And he should know that his fiancée is missing."

"Assuming your memory is correct and they *did* get engaged."

"True."

"For that we'll need to find a computer and do a search." He frowned and looked down, then off into the distance.

People had started to fill the tables around them. Joshua's gaze sharpened. He looked around, stared at the passing traffic, then abruptly stood. "Let's go. I have something to tell you and…this is not the place." He tossed some bills on the table, helped her up and opened the Jeep door for her.

She somehow didn't think this confession of his would be good. And she wasn't ready for more bad news.

He got in, started the engine and headed north.

"Where are we going?" If she was able to distract him, maybe he wouldn't tell her something she didn't want to hear.

"Spokane. They've made my truck and possibly this Jeep if they got a glimpse of it at your place. I need to switch vehicles."

"Why not switch vehicles here?"

"Car rentals in these small towns are all outdoors and super easy to check with just a drive-by. I also need to find a safe place to leave you."

Bile rose in her throat. "No."

"What do you mean, no?"

"I know who and what you are. And you're not leaving me anywhere."

Joshua gripped the steering wheel. "What do you think I am?"

"I saw the pelts in your hidden closet. I recognized a Canadian lynx, an endangered species, along with the animal traps. You're breaking the law. A poacher."

Her words cut him to the core. That had been his goal for his investigation, but he didn't want Bethany to think he was a criminal. He touched his tags, then glanced over at her.

Her face was flushed and she'd twisted in her seat to stare directly at him.

"If you believe I'm a criminal, then you should be happy I'm dropping you off and getting out of your life." His voice was husky. "Why would you want to stay with me?"

"Because..." Now her voice was unsteady. She took a deep, shuddering breath. "Even though you're breaking the law, in here..." she placed a hand over her heart "...I believe in you."

He almost swerved off the road. *This can't happen.* Now more than ever, he had to convince Bethany that it wasn't safe for her and that he wasn't sure he could keep her from harm. Not only were the people after her dangerous, his own investigation into illegal hunting could put her at risk if the poachers wanted to use her as leverage. "Don't." His voice was deliberately harsh. "You need to work out what's happening to you.

Do research online, make some phone calls, and be someplace safe while you do that. And I need to get back to…my work." He hated himself as he said it. Out of the corner of his eye, he saw her stiffen and stare straight ahead.

They drove silently for miles through the rolling, wheat-stubble fields, remote farmhouses and passing small towns dominated by grain elevators.

He couldn't leave it like this. "Bethany—"

"I know why you're doing this."

He glanced at her.

She'd once again turned to him. "You're worried about my safety. You're trying to protect me. But just keeping me from harm won't give me back my sister. My aunt. My home. My life. You don't know what will trigger my memory, what becomes important, what is a clue, and what is simply…background noise. I need to be actively involved. So I'm afraid you're stuck with me."

Joshua couldn't look at her, afraid his face would betray the longing stirring inside him. Bethany was beautiful, her presence sinking deep into his heart, and he didn't want to let her go. But she was vulnerable, trapped in a dangerous mess, and he feared she didn't feel the same spark he did. Worse, being near him might pull her deeper into harm's way. The thought twisted in his chest: *I want you here, but you're safer far from me.* Torn, he forced his voice steady. "I can handle this alone. You need to stay somewhere safe. When this is over…"

"This is nonnegotiable."

"Nothing is nonnegotiable."

"Ha! Then you haven't met one of the bullheaded, stubborn, determined Hall sisters."

"Did you just remember that?"

"It seems to fit, don't you think?"

"In that case, you might as well get out that notebook and start working on a plan of action."

She gave a short nod and her lips tightened as if she were hiding a smile.

He loosened his white-knuckled grip on the steering wheel.

She pulled out the Walmart bag that served as her purse and suitcase, lifted the spiral bound notebook and opened it. She'd written each entry on a separate line. She read the entries out loud. "We know the last word on the list—pierce—is the town of Pierce where I went with my sister. And the old building was the historical building." She jotted a few notes. "And we found the café in Pullman."

"Where does your sister live?" The heavy brick he'd had in his chest had lifted.

"Boise." She tapped the pad with her pen. "Right. Ruth wasn't local and had to have been visiting me when we made this trip. I have…had all the family records, such as they were, at my house. We were probably going through them and decided to travel to Pierce."

"What about a timeline?"

"Good idea. I know the weather was cool, so probably spring or fall."

"You already figured the Orofino Lumberjack Days was your festival. Fall. Do you think the trip to Pierce was on that same trip?"

"Yes. I'd say so. All those memories are jumbled together."

For what felt like the hundredth time, Joshua checked to be sure they weren't followed.

"Anyone following us?"

Joshua shook his head. "I'm probably being paranoid."

"I'd say cautious."

They were reaching the outskirts of Spokane and traffic had picked up. "After we get a rental truck," Joshua said, "we'll take Izzy for a walk, then swing by the library to use their computer."

The vehicle exchange went smoothy, Izzy enjoyed stretching her legs at a rest stop, but the information they found in the library computer left them reeling.

Like Bethany, there were no apparent records of Ruth Ann Hall. Nor Nan Hall, Bethany's aunt. "How can that be? How can three people be deleted?"

Joshua drummed his fingers on the computer table. "Usually they can't. For someone like you who lives alone and works remotely, you don't have that many connections to be severed. What kind of work did your sister do?"

"She was between jobs, but she'd been a nanny to a family in Seattle."

"Maybe we could contact—"

Bethany shook her head. "They moved out of the country. That's why she was between jobs. And I guess Aunt Nan was just as easy to delete. She sold jelly at farmers markets and festivals."

Joshua took the notebook from Bethany's hand, turned the page and wrote, *Thorough, well-funded, tech savvy, calculating, cunning, ruthless. Possibly willing to kill.* "This is what we're up against. Are you sure you want to continue?"

"Yes." She smiled, but it didn't reach her eyes. "Let's look for Daniel Adams."

The name brought pages of hits on Google and hundreds on social media. Bethany added a PhD to the name, but still too many potential Daniel Adamses came up.

"Do you know a middle name?" Joshua asked.

"Roy." She typed in the name. "Eureka. He did teach economics at WSU. Last December, he was hired by EarthKind, Incorporated." She searched for their web page and read their mission statement. "'EarthKind is dedicated to discovering natural solutions to issues faced by adults and to putting them on the road to a healthy lifestyle.'"

"'Natural' is good—"

"Arsenic is natural." She clicked on the location tab. "It's in Minneapolis." She slumped. "Dead end."

Bethany wrote down the corporate phone number anyway, but she knew this was probably futile. "If my sister was engaged to Dr. Adams, which I have a vague memory of, I don't think they're still engaged."

"Why do you say that?"

"Shhhhhhh." A woman at a nearby computer glared at them.

They both stood and left, heading for the rental truck. "Why don't you think they're still engaged?" Joshua asked again.

"This trip, the one I was taking with Ruth to visit Aunt Nan… I don't know…it's just a feeling I have, not really a memory…but I think we were reconciling."

He unlocked the truck door and opened it for her. "Over Dr. Adams being engaged to both of you?"

"That would be a good reason, don't you think? The words *Never again. Shattered trust doesn't mend* keep repeating in my head. Having my fiancé break up and become engaged to my sister would make for bad relations. It totally fits the facts that I've discovered."

He paused as if he wanted to say something, then shut the door behind her and got into the driver's seat.

Bethany rubbed her face. Her head pounded. "Do you think we could stop somewhere so I can get some aspirin?"

"Sure." He drove a few blocks, pulled into a drugstore and parked in the shade next to a row of trees.

She found the pain relief aisle quickly enough and grabbed a small generic bottle.

Joshua nudged her, then showed her a bottle labeled Memoreon. "Maybe you should buy this to help your memory. It says it's a patented formula, up to one hundred percent effective, and clinically tested."

She took the bottle, then snorted. "A patent doesn't mean it works, only that it's unique. And *up* to one hundred percent effective could be zero percent And finally, clinically tested? It could have failed every trial." She handed it back.

"I see your snarky side is returning."

"And apparently I have a cynical bent as well."

"Or maybe you became cynical after your breakup. Shattered trust."

They picked up a six-pack of bottled water along with a bag of dog food and disposable bowls for Izzy. All the while Bethany mulled over Joshua's observation. *Or possibly my cynicism caused the rift.*

Back at the car, they stayed in the shade while Bethany downed several aspirin, then fed and watered Izzy. She leaned against the truck, watching the dog eat.

Joshua joined her, but his gaze never left the street beside them. "Bethany, these people that are after you, trying to kill you…do you have any new memories or insight into why?"

"No. I don't have money or power. It can't be love, revenge or jealousy. I don't know anything, so secrets or cover-ups don't fit—"

"That you know of. But what if it *is* one of those reasons, but you can't remember?"

"Maybe."

He stiffened, staring at something.

Bethany followed his gaze.

A black pickup was cruising slowly past, then turned into the parking lot.

Her stomach lurched and she pushed off the truck.

As it passed, she saw an elderly man in a ball cap behind the wheel. He parked near the store.

Bethany let out a breath she didn't realize she was holding.

Izzy finished devouring her kibble and had drained the disposable bowl of water twice. She looked at the grass under the trees, then at Bethany.

Bethany waved her on. "Okay, go ahead and hit the doggie

loo." She turned to Joshua. "We know these people have gone to great lengths to erase Ruth, Nan and me. I'm going to assume all the big things like driver's licenses, internet presence and so on have disappeared on them as well. But what about the small things?"

"I'm listening."

"I was thinking about that festival where Aunt Nan was selling jelly. Wouldn't she need to pay for her booth? There would be a record of that. And our visit to the historical building in Pierce. I'm pretty sure I signed the guest book."

"What would that prove?"

"That I'm me. You have no idea how…frightening it is to have no provable identity. And look how much information we got from the café. I *was* engaged. The name and job of my former fiancé. The more these small memories come together with concrete facts, the more I can put this puzzle together. I can go to the police, maybe the FBI. Nan and Ruth have been missing for at least two days now."

"You think we should drive to Orofino and Pierce."

"Yes."

"They'll be watching for us."

"Yes. But I doubt they'd think I'd dive directly into the lion's den, and maybe we can outsmart them."

Joshua rubbed his lower lip for a moment. "How?"

"You're growing a beard at a remarkably fast rate."

Joshua absently scratched his chin.

"And, please don't be offended, but your scar is almost invisible. You look very different." *And very easy to look at.* The thought startled Bethany.

"Do you like this look?"

"Yes!" The word came out far more enthusiastically than she'd wanted. She looked down at Izzy, picked up her food and water bowls, and stuck them into a plastic bag. She hoped the heat burning her face would have chilled by the time she looked back at Joshua.

He reached over to her and cradled her face in his calloused hand. "And what about your pretty face?"

The air around her seemed to thin and she had trouble catching her breath. "I…um…my hair… I could…" Her mind went completely blank.

He let go, but his hand briefly stroked her hair. "Right." Now his voice was rough. He cleared his throat. "Since we'll be focusing our research in Clearwater County, we should stay in the area to save time. We'll stop by a store on the way to Orofino, get provisions and whatever you need to do to change your appearance, then camp out at my—"

"Your…?"

"It's my place, my house in town."

"What were you about to say? Family home? Vacation house? Summer place? Crash pad? Safe house?"

He ignored her questions. "We need to get going."

Joshua chose the most direct route south, figuring on a stop in Lewiston, Idaho. It was less than an hour from there to his place in town.

Before they got to Lewiston, he pulled off the highway to a dirt road. He drove up the road for a mile or so, kicking up clouds of dust, before turning around and returning to the highway.

"Did you need something or…?" Bethany asked.

"Nothing stands out more around here than a sparkling-clean car or truck. We need to blend in."

After a brief stop at a Lewiston store for provisions, they resumed their journey.

By the time they were on the picturesque highway paralleling the Clearwater River, long blue shadows had plunged the river valley into dusk. The closer they got to their destination, the more alert he'd become. His gaze constantly flickered between the rearview mirror and the road ahead.

"Where do you think they are?" Bethany asked in a quiet voice.

"I'm guessing they've split up and sent at least one person to see if we show up at my ranch. Possibly a second person or another team watching the roads. They've probably found my truck and trailer by now. They know we took off in a hurry and would have limited resources, so would probably stick to places we know."

"What about a hotel or—"

"Too easy to find strangers. I need to get to my house in Orofino, but it's a small town, so they know we'll be in either the Jeep or another rig. They'll be watching every vehicle on the road."

"How will we get past them?"

"I'm going on a back road that hopefully they're not aware of, but we still have to stay on the main road for a bit. Just to be safe, you're going to hop in the back and lay low. If they do spot us, all they should see is a single man in a baseball hat driving a dusty truck." He said a silent prayer.

She pulled something out of her shopping bag and bent over it. She gave a quiet grunt, then said, "Here," and handed him a pair of oversize, tortoiseshell rimmed glasses. "Can you see?"

"No."

She took them back and popped out the lenses. "No one should be able to see there's no glass in them."

He put them on.

He could feel her gaze on him.

"That definitely works. Now slump a bit."

He rounded his shoulders and slid down in his seat.

"Perfect."

"Now you. Time to disappear. I'm coming up on the turn."

She unsnapped her seat belt. "You first, Izzy." She hoisted the dog into the back seat, then followed.

Just in time. Parked at the turnoff from the highway was the white van.

He kept his eyes straight ahead as he signaled to turn, then turned left. He could almost feel the burning gaze of the driver. If it were still the woman from Bethany's house, she shouldn't recognize him.

He gripped the steering wheel, his hands clammy against the leather wrapping. The truck felt like a furnace. Sweat formed under the rim of his cap.

He drove carefully, keeping his head straight while he checked in his rearview mirror. He didn't relax his grip until he'd turned another corner and saw no vehicle following him.

"That was the white van." He turned his head so she could hear over the truck's engine. "Stay down a bit longer just in case they have other lookouts."

He entered town by a back road, which would make him appear as if he was coming from a different direction. He quickly turned into his garage. "We're here."

Bethany straightened, then groaned. "Time for more aspirin."

He got out, helped Izzy and her from the back seat, then led her to the rear of the house and unlocked the door. "Give me a minute before you turn on any lights." Using the dim illumination from a distant streetlight, he went from room to room, closing blackout curtains. By the time he was done, the house was plunged into total darkness. Only then did he switch on the lights.

Bethany and Izzy were still waiting in the kitchen.

"Let me get you that aspirin. You go sit or lay down on the sofa." He nodded toward the next room. "I'll unload the truck."

Her face was pinched and pale in the overhead light and she nodded and shuffled into the living room. He brought her the bottle and a glass of water, then left her to get the stuff from the truck.

By the time he'd brought everything in and put them away, she'd stretched out on the leather sofa and was sleeping. Izzy sprawled next to her on the sofa and quietly snored.

He watched them for a few moments. They looked so peaceful he simply draped a blanket over them. He had a feeling the next few days would be anything but.

SEVEN

Bethany opened her eyes, then blinked. It took her a moment to figure out where she was. Joshua's living room sofa. She had a soft blanket over her and a pillow smelling faintly of lavender under her head. Both undoubtedly provided by Joshua after she'd crashed the night before. The living room opened to an older kitchen with a terracotta tile floor, hickory cabinets and a farmhouse sink. A white table and two chairs sat in the middle of the room.

The blackout curtains were open and early morning light peeked between closed horizontal blinds.

The tantalizing aroma of fresh coffee filled the air.

She stirred, and Izzy, tucked under the blanket behind her bent legs, grunted. Bethany pulled the blanket off and sat up. Izzy stretched out, apparently content to sleep in. Bethany covered the dog, leaving her head exposed, and then stood.

Her body reminded her she'd been in a car accident, dumped off a horse, climbed a mountain, and been tied up in her own home. She went in search of the aspirin bottle.

Joshua stepped into the kitchen from outside. His dark hair was tousled, his beard rough and untamed. He wore a dark olive vest over a weathered, plaid flannel shirt. "Good. You're awake." Without asking, he grabbed the aspirin bottle and handed it to her.

"I look that bad?" She took it.

"You look wonderful—" He pivoted and made a show of rummaging through the cabinet to find her a coffee mug.

She reflexively finger-combed her hair and rolled her lips to keep the grin at bay. Taking the proffered mug, she filled it with water to wash down the pills, then poured coffee into it. She tried not to look at Joshua, but she was aware of him. She sat at the table.

Before she could ask, he placed a spoon, sugar bowl and a carton of half-and-half in front of her. "Are you okay with scrambled eggs and toast?"

"Sounds wonderful." She looked around the room, trying to get a feel for why he needed to maintain two places, why a safe house? She didn't like the possibilities that swarmed her brain. *Drugs. Poaching. Part of some kind of militia group.* But that didn't fit with someone who'd rescued her from a burning car, then a group of mountain men, then the thugs who'd abducted her.

"Did you want to go to Pierce first, or start here?"

His comment interrupted her troubling thoughts. "Here. Who do you think might have a list of the vendors during the festival?"

"There's a festival committee, but they'd probably run the paperwork through the city as they'd need a street vendor license. City hall opens at eight."

"Will you be coming with me?"

"No. They're looking for a man and woman. I'll stay nearby to be sure you're safe."

Her fingers tightened around the mug, grounding her as his words sank in. Each syllable of his concern breached her carefully constructed defenses, stirring that longing she wasn't ready to name, a pull toward him that felt as dangerous as it was inevitable.

After breakfast she grabbed some of the purchases from the day before and disappeared into the bathroom. She'd mentally gone through all the ways she could alter her appearance and had settled on this one. When she'd finished, she took stock in the mirror. Her reddish-brown hair was now silvery gray that she rolled into a bun at her neck. She applied a foundation a bit lighter than her normal, then used contour cream to hollow out her cheeks and around her eyes to make them look more sunken. She'd purchased an oversize gray cardigan sweater that she put over her jeans and a long-sleeved T-shirt. She added dark-rimmed glasses, took one last look at her reflection, and stepped into the kitchen.

Joshua turned to look at her. His eyes widened and mouth dropped.

"Land-o-lakes, sonny, don't just stand there providing your mouth as a bird house." She shuffled forward. "Let's get this-here production on the road."

"Amazing." Joshua dropped into a chair. "I'm getting a preview of fifty years from now."

She grinned in spite of herself. "Listen, you young whipper-snapper, you think you're gonna remember me in fifty years?"

"I suspect I'll never forget you."

They stared at each other, his words hanging between them in the silent room.

Bethany was the first to break eye contact. She looked at the table. He'd set it with denim blue and cream stoneware and added some flowers to a small vase in the center of the table. "W-where did you find the flowers?"

"They grow wild around here." He turned and popped some bread into the toaster.

She was able to steady herself while his back was turned. She knew that scent. It had a connection to a still-missing part of her memory.

Joshua placed a plate of scrambled eggs in front of her. The sliced toast framed her meal, already spread with a dark purple jelly. She picked up a slice and sniffed.

Joshua joined her at the table with his own plate. "I'm sorry. I didn't think. I already put some preserves on your toast. I'll make you—"

"No, no. That's fine. What did you put on the toast?"

"Butter and huckleberry preserves."

"I thought huckleberries were more red."

"Nope. Dark purple."

"So…not the color. It must be the smell."

"Smell?"

"For some reason, this smell is connected to a memory. A bad memory."

Joshua frowned down at his toast for a moment. "Do you think that's somehow important?"

"I don't know. I'm just so tired of having these big holes in my memory…"

"Well, hopefully today we can fill more of your past in. I'll drive you over to the city hall—"

"Are you sure you won't come in with me?"

Joshua thought for a moment. He hated lying to her, so he settled on a half-truth. "Even though you look quite a bit different, we need to be ultra careful. Anyway, I have an errand to run."

She raised her eyebrows but didn't ask.

After they finished eating, she took care of Izzy while he cleaned up. He kept glancing at her fussing over the dog. His mind drifted, picturing her at his ranch, caring for his animals.

Caring for him.

How would she handle his dangerous life? *Why* should she be exposed to it? He scratched his chin. He couldn't do that. He'd have to decide between the work he loved, the critically important job he did, and her.

And he wasn't sure she'd want him to do that. He wasn't even sure she cared that much.

She caught him staring at her. "What's that look for?"

"Nothing. Do you think Izzy will be okay to leave alone for a bit?"

"You mean, will she destroy your house while we're gone? She'll be fine. But—"

"But you'd rather have her with you. You do realize she's a uniquely identifiable dog?"

"Is that a polite way of saying she's—"

"I would *never* say she's ugly."

"She's perfect." She kissed the dog on the head.

"For a dog with no hunting, tracking or guarding skills, agreed." He strolled to the window and checked for anyone lurking nearby. "We'll take Izzy and I'll keep her with me in the truck. Ready?"

"As I'll ever be."

They hurried to the garage. The trees lining the street and on either side of the house isolated it from the neighbors, but he wasn't taking any chances.

They didn't speak until he'd pulled up to the curb in front of city hall. "I won't be long on my errand. If you finish first, wait on that bench, but…um…"

"Don't worry. I'll stay alert." She reached out and touched his arm before jumping out of the truck.

He could still feel her warm hand five minutes later when he parked in front of the post office. As he walked up to the counter, the postmaster's eyes widened. Joshua handed him the postcard and the man left, returning quickly with the package containing the satellite phone. He glanced quickly around the room, then whispered, "I thought you had to keep your head down. Did they uncover the mole in the department?"

Joshua's head snapped up. "No. How did you—"

Several customers came into the lobby.

Joshua took the package out to his pickup, then drove to the back of the building and out of sight. A dog barked in the distance and Izzy raised her head, then went back to sleep. A colorful grocery store flyer slid across the road in the slight breeze. He stared down at the phone in his lap. He had a slim hope that he'd get backup help. His old boss wouldn't have hesitated to dive in, look up the information he needed, contact the right people. But this new man was by-the-book straight—and didn't like this undercover work. He'd made it clear that his staff had to keep their heads down and do their work, or else.

His boss picked up on the second ring. "I hope you're calling me to say you've arrested the poachers who've been trapping endangered game."

"No. I need help on another matter—"

"Joshua, there are no other matters." His voice was harsh. "We haven't found the source of leaks and this phone call may have thrown your whole investigation out the window."

"By any chance, did you ever tell the postmaster here who I am?"

"Of course not."

"You might just look for a link between him and your mole."

"I'll make note of it."

"But the real reason I'm calling is I think there's something really big going on around here."

"Big like what?"

"Kidnapping. Burglary. Attempted murder—"

"Then it's not your job. That's for local law enforcement. Call it in on a tip line and then stay out of it. We've spent too much time and money on setting you up undercover to blow it all now. Drop this immediately."

Joshua's jaw clenched. An anonymous tip about the scum chasing them would be easy. A quick call, and he'd be free. Free from the risk of blowing his cover, free from choosing between his badge and her. She might even be safer without him, without his baggage.

He'd never be able to explain his work to her anyway. The work that kept him up at night, tracking poachers through snow-choked forests to save the endangered Canadian lynx, the caribou, anything that gave his life meaning after the accident. The crash that took his wife and son. His chest tightened at the memory, a dull ache that never left.

But the thought of leaving Bethany hollowed him out. She'd trusted him, leaned on him through the wreckage of her erased life.

He pulled the tags from under his shirt and rubbed his thumb over the surface. Shouldn't his earlier life be enough to last him?

Walk away, and she'd be alone, always glancing over her shoulder for the next threat. These people could vanish, only to resurface when she least expected it.

His heart thudded, heavy with the truth he couldn't shake. He didn't want to leave her—not now, maybe not ever.

"Do you hear me?"

"Yes, sir, but I can't—"

"Then you leave me no choice. I'm calling you in and shutting down your operation. Report to my office tomorrow morning at 0800. I'm assigning you to desk duties for the foreseeable future."

Joshua stared straight ahead. "And if I don't show up?"

"Then collect your pink slip when you finally do." *Click.*

Joshua slowly lowered the phone, then repackaged it and returned it to the postmaster without comment. There were several people around, so Joshua got in and out as swiftly as he could. It was less than three blocks to city hall. Bethany was seated on the bench in front. She spotted him, then deliberately turned her head and looked left. He was about to beep the horn in case she didn't remember the truck, when he saw what she'd been looking at.

The black truck was parked a block away in front of a restaurant.

He signaled, turned into an alley halfway up the street, then took a right into a parking lot and waited. Hopefully she saw him dodge into the side street and would figure out his plan.

He slumped in his seat and watched every passing vehicle. Just when he was trying to figure out how he could look for her, Bethany appeared, walking up the street with a convincingly elderly gait. She veered toward him as soon as she spotted the truck. She ran the last few steps and jumped in. "I spotted them just before I left the building." She was breathless. "I had no way to warn you."

"You did great."

"So did you." She smiled, but her lips were tight. "Let's get out of here."

"Pierce?"

"Pierce."

Joshua drove a wide berth around where the men were having lunch and they were soon climbing out of the river valley toward the tiny hamlet of Pierce.

"What did you find out at city hall?" he asked her once they were some distance from town.

"I went in and asked for a vendor form for the festival. I said I'd heard good things about it. The clerk was very sweet and excited about the event. She said they were very picky—everyone had to be vetted."

"Interesting. What does that mean?"

"It means first priority went to Idaho residents and they had to have an Idaho driver's license, which they checked. I asked her if I could contact anyone who'd been a vendor in the past for their experiences with the event. She gave me a printout of participants." She reached in a pocket and pulled out a piece of paper. "Nan Hall wasn't listed as a vendor, but there was a Nancy Temming. I asked her about a couple of the names, what they sold and so on." She took a gulp of air. "She said Nancy Temming sold preserves—huckleberry preserves." She looked at Joshua. "Aunt Nan lied to us." She held up the piece of paper. "Her name isn't Nan Hall. It's Nancy Temming."

Bethany could still feel the cold rush she'd experienced when she heard about the difference in names. What else wasn't real? She clutched the armrest in an attempt to ground herself. To stop her mind from floating, untethered, seeking something concrete, real.

"Bethany? Hello?"

She finally registered Joshua speaking to her. "Sorry." She let go of the armrest and touched Izzy. The dog responded by licking her hand. *Izzy is real. Joshua is real. The scent of pine trees coming through the window is real.*

"Are you okay?"

"Not really."

"Let's bring you back to earth. How did you find your aunt in the first place? You told me you and your sister met your aunt at the festival a year ago. Did you find out you were related there?"

"No. Um. We..." She rubbed her head, trying to press all the cotton wool from her memory. "We went to Pierce first because we had information that some of our family had homesteaded there during the gold rush of the 1860s. The Pierce Historic Courthouse had photos of some of the early settlers. I remember signing the guest book. And the smell of age. And a really chatty woman...named... Agatha? Agnes? Something like that. She said there was at least one member of the family still living in the area. We got excited to meet her. I think she was the one who mentioned the festival and that Nan—that's the name she said—Nan would be selling her preserves there. She said we should get there early because Nan's preserves sold out quickly. I know we went to another museum nearby, then drove to Orofino and introduced ourselves."

"We need to find this Agnes or Agatha and see what she remembers."

Bethany pulled out her spiral notebook and opened to her original notes. *Parade. People in plaid shirts. Flannel shirts? Popcorn.* She added *Orofino Lumberjack Days.*

The next entry, *old, unpainted wooden building,* and *Pierce* answered itself.

Floating in an inner tube down a cold river on a hot day.

Outdoor café smelling of coffee. Were probably connected with her fiancé.

Joshua had written on the next page, *Thorough, well-funded, tech savvy, calculating, cunning, ruthless. Possibly willing to kill.*

She could see no connection with anything in her own life. "Joshua, let me read what we've written and let's just brainstorm some ideas." She read her notes to him.

"Mistaken identity?" he posited when she'd finished. "Something in Nan's background? Something in your sister's background?"

"Good." She started to write. "Uncovered some information? Blackmail? Maybe my family found a gold mine and they're just looking for family members?" Her chuckle caught in her throat. That would be so very simple.

"Don't you wish. What if you saw something important—something you weren't supposed to see—and didn't even know it?"

Bethany grimaced. "And they don't know that I have holes in my memory. Maybe I crossed paths with the wrong people?"

"Could someone in your family have left you something? Money, land, something valuable?"

Bethany continued to write. "Nan lied about her name. Maybe she had ties to someone dangerous."

"Or you're really a spy. Undercover for the mafia." Joshua smiled as he said it, then grew quiet.

They'd reached a sign at the edge of town that said, Welcome to Pierce, Where Idaho First Began. The commercial buildings were spread out and a hodgepodge of styles in this town of barely five hundred souls. Some of the log buildings looked as if a line of saddled horses wouldn't be out of place.

"I've never visited here," Joshua said.

"It's not exactly on your way to anyplace. Go slow. I think—yes. Up there on the right. Turn there."

Joshua did as directed. The courthouse's simple, untreated wooden siding was stained shades of brown umber to sepia, a reminder of decades long past. The sign in front informed them that the building was only open by appointment and directed them to the Logging Museum back on Main Street.

Bethany swallowed down the prickly feeling that threatened to overcome her. *Will this hold answers, or just be another dead end?* And what would they do next if this didn't hold some answers?

They turned around and returned to Main. Once parked in front of the museum, Joshua remained still, his gaze sweeping the street.

Bethany rolled down the window for Izzy and got out. She stretched to try and get the stiffness out of her body, but it didn't help.

Joshua joined her and together they entered the museum.

"Howdy." A plump, middle-aged woman approached. "Welcome to the Logging Museum."

"Thank you." Bethany tried to smile but her lips were tight. "I…um…was here, well, maybe not *here*…about a year ago and met a woman named Agnes or Agatha or—"

"Do you mean Alma? Yes, Alma Stevens. I'd just moved here and met her. Poor woman."

A gray fog settled over Bethany. "Why 'poor woman'?"

"Oh, dear, it was March. March seventeenth to be exact. Right after we had the break-in. Or was it before the break-in? It was all so very chaotic—"

"But why did you call her 'poor woman'?" Bethany tried to make her voice less sharp, but the woman gave her a quick flicker of her eyebrow.

"Alma was in a car accident. She went off the road. No one could believe it. Everyone said Alma was such a good driver. Very slow and methodical. They didn't find her for…well, it was all so distressing. I came here to get away from such things."

Another dead end. Bethany slumped.

"Did you say you were here before?" The woman was staring at Bethany's gray hair. "You look so familiar. Maybe your daughter?"

"She…um…was here maybe a year ago." Bethany moved away from the woman's sharp stare.

"What about the break-in?" Joshua asked.

"Some people think that's why Alma got careless driving. Because she was upset that the courthouse was robbed. I blame the kids. No respect. No discipline—"

"And I'm guessing no arrests were made." Joshua didn't wait for the woman's reply. "What was taken?"

"Nothing of great value. Some photographs, a diary. Shameful, that's what it was. Just shameful. Hooligans—"

"Was there any damage?"

The woman sniffed. "Tore some pages out of the guest book."

"And the diary? What do you know about that?"

"It belonged to Ida Mae McPherson Hall, an early settler."

Bethany blinked as the fog cleared around another memory. *And my great-great-grandmother.*

"Thank you very much for the information," Joshua told the docent. "We have to head out—"

"Don't you want to look around the museum?" the woman asked.

"Not right now. We'll come back." He took Bethany's arm and left the museum before the woman could say anything else. They returned to the truck where Izzy greeted them like they'd been gone for a month. "What's wrong? You just turned pale."

"Ida Mae is my great-great-grandmother and she wrote that diary. But more than that. There's a flyer on that message center. It shows my picture and offers a reward if anyone has seen me. That's why I looked a bit familiar to that woman, even with this disguise. Those horrible men must have emailed it to all of the businesses in Pierce—"

"Get in. It will only be a matter of time before she spots the flyer, puts it together and makes the call." Joshua turned the truck around and started driving out of town.

"Wait," Bethany said. "If we leave now, we won't have any answers." She gave him a pleading look. "My face is on the flyer, but not yours. Let's see if anyone has lived around here and knows about the history."

"Those men will be on the road the second someone calls."

"So let's set a timer. If the docent called right after we left, what would be the soonest those goons could get here?"

"Maybe an hour or less."

"So we need to be out of here in an hour. Okay?"

He stopped the truck. "That doesn't give us much time." He turned and looked back at the small town. "What's the best place for gossip?"

"Beauty salon, but you'll stand out too much in there." Bethany turned around as well. "There's a café. Go in and flash that cute smile at the waitress—"

"You like my smile?"

Bethany blushed.

He quickly reversed the truck and shot over to the café. "Wait here and stay alert."

When he entered the café, the aroma of fried chicken and burgers filled the air and Joshua's stomach grumbled.

A teenage waitress immediately spotted him and picked up a menu. "Welcome to Pierce Café. How many?"

"I'm not sure I can stay." He smiled at her.

She fumbled the menu. "Oh. What, like, brings you here?"

"I'm doing some family research. Do you happen to know anyone in town who knows a lot about the history?"

"You mean, like, the museum?"

"Apparently the docent there is relatively new to this area."

Joshua leaned a little closer. "Maybe someone who's lived here a long time?"

"Hmm. Well, the folk who've been here the longest, like, are all over at the cemetery." She giggled at her own wit. "Still living, I guess, would be ole Miss Hutton. She's, like, a fossil. At least fifty. Maybe older."

"Where does this fossil live?" Joshua kept a straight face.

The waitress took out a pen from her utility apron and drew on a paper napkin. "Go up the street to the blue house, only it's, like, white now and not really a house. Turn right. Go, like, three or four streets, turn right again and look for a house with a metal roof and lots of firewood."

"Thank you." He tried not to run back to the truck but he was eager to find this ole Miss Hutton and be on the road before the thugs met up with them again. He could almost feel their hot breath on his neck.

"Did you get a name?" Bethany asked him when he got in the truck.

"Yup. And an address." Well, sort of, he added silently. He started the truck and drove up the street.

"Do you think this diary contains information on what we talked about before? Something about land or money?"

He shrugged. "Could be. Maybe a map, or something illegal that no one wants to come to light."

"Or a confession about a love in her life?"

He flashed her a grin. "So, the romantic side of you is coming out." He snapped his mouth shut, instantly regretting his words.

Bethany's cheeks flamed. "Um…it's probably just pages and pages of who was kissing who in 1932…" The blush deepened, she glanced at him, then immediately down at her lap. "I mean…okay…how about her award-winning, secret cake recipe?"

"If you say so." As confusing as the waitress's directions were, her map was spot-on and he found the house. It was surrounded by broken-down cars, a sled, two lawn mowers and the promised stack of firewood. Bethany was the first out of the truck, carrying her notebook as she trotted to the front door. By the time Joshua had joined her, an older woman in a faded housedress opened the door.

"I'm not buying anything." She was about to close the door when Bethany blurted out, "We're here to talk to Miss Hutton about the missing diary of Ida Mae McPherson Hall."

The woman paused. "Why?"

"She was my great-great-grandmother."

"I'm Evelyn Hutton. Come in." She opened the door wider.

Bethany glanced over her shoulder at Joshua and whispered, "Forty-eight minutes."

EIGHT

Bethany stepped into the house. On her left was a living room that didn't look like too much living had occurred there. The furniture was old, dark and uncomfortable-looking. On the right was a kitchen with avocado-colored appliances, white-painted cupboards and gold-laminated countertops. Beyond the kitchen was an oversize dining room with a picnic table partly covered with a plastic red-and-white tablecloth and surrounded by various colored, webbed lawn chairs. White storage boxes and tired-looking cardboard boxes lined the walls to the level of the windows. A computer and printer sat on a small wooden desk in the corner. The air smelled musty, with an underlying odor of dirty cat litter.

Evelyn waved them into the dining room. "Take a load off. Coffee?"

"No, thank you." Bethany pulled out a lawn chair, placed the notebook on the table and sat facing the kitchen. Joshua chose a seat at the end of the table. "I'm fine as well," he said.

Evelyn poured herself a cup and sat opposite Bethany. "So. Your family goes back quite a ways here. I'm writing a book about it." She waved toward the boxes. "Been working on it for years. Alma was helping me. She loaned me some letters, papers, photos…" She took a sip of coffee, then cradled the mug and stared unfocused at the table.

Bethany stole a glance at her watch. She didn't want to interrupt the woman, but after an awkward silence, she cleared her throat.

"Yes. Right." Evelyn stood, found a smudged pair of glasses on the table, then moved to a set of boxes stacked next to the computer. "Hall, MacPherson, let's see," she said under her breath. After rearranging several, she pulled out a tattered cardboard box and placed it on the table. "I read your great-great-granny's diary."

Bethany glanced at Joshua, then leaned forward. "And…?"

Evelyn began rummaging around in the box. She paused. "And? And what? It was just that, a diary of an average woman living in the boonies. I have some notes." She pulled out a small stack of yellow lined paper with cramped writing on it. "Yes. Here." She skimmed a few pages. "Uh-huh. Right."

Bethany wanted to scream at her, snatch the paper from her hands, dive into the box on her own. She deliberately pulled a pen from her pocket and opened the notebook, making an effort to not stab the paper.

"Okay, I remember more now." Evelyn looked over her glasses. "Ida Mae, daughter of Elias Hall and Ann MacPherson, was born in 1901. She married Howard Hall in…let's see…1921."

Bethany wrote as quickly as she could.

"They had two children, Edward and Ida Mae."

"Wait," Joshua said. "I thought you said Ida Mae was the mother."

"Ida Mae named her daughter the same name. But she called her Nan."

The small hairs on Bethany's arm prickled. "Nan Hall?"

"Yes. Sure. I have a photo somewhere in here." She looked further, finally pulling out a faded, black-and-white photo of a woman in a print housedress standing with two children, a boy in overalls and a girl in a print dress with an oversize bow in her hair.

"Anyway," Evelyn continued. "Edward married—"

Bethany had circled the name in her notebook. "What happened to Nan?"

"I don't rightly remember. I do have another photo or two in here." She put down her notes and pulled a bunch of photos out. Most were mounted on cardboard and had names on the back written in faded ink.

Bethany wanted to urge Evelyn to look faster, but she didn't want the woman to get angry. Again she glanced at her watch, noted how long they'd been here and felt her anxiety deepen.

"Ah, here you go." Evelyn handed Bethany two photographs of a woman. The first was slightly blurry and showed her standing in front of a white house wearing a dark, broad-shouldered, nipped-in-waist dress with a white collar. Her hair was wavy and tucked behind her ears. On the back of the photo, it read, *Ida Mae (Nan) Hall, July 1943.* The second was a studio photograph, possibly a class photo.

The woman in the photos was the spitting image of Aunt Nan.

The photo dropped from Bethany's numb fingers. The room was suddenly too warm and a loud buzzing sounded in her ears. *Impossible.* That would make Aunt Nan over a hundred years old.

Joshua was beside her, though she hadn't seen him move.

"Is she all right?" Evelyn asked, her voice coming from a long distance.

"She was in a car accident recently." Joshua took her hand and cradled it. "Could you bring her a glass of water?"

A glass was shoved into her hand and Joshua released her other one so she could hold the glass more securely. "Thank you." She gulped the water, then carefully returned it to the table. She picked up the close-up photo and studied it carefully. It looked identical to Aunt Nan, down to the small brown birthmark on her chin. "This is impossible." She handed the photo to Joshua. "This is a photo of my aunt Nan. Or the woman calling herself Aunt Nan."

Joshua took the photo, studied it, then turned it over and read the back. "How old did you say your aunt should be?"

"Forties?"

Evelyn was looking back and forth between them. "I don't understand."

"You and me both." Bethany indicated the photo. "I'm looking into the mystery of a woman calling herself Nan Hall."

"Ooh, I love mysteries. Maybe we can look into it on my computer. I just got it and my nephew set it up. I'm not sure how—"

"That would be awesome." Bethany stood, then grabbed the table to steady herself.

"Let me do it." Joshua pulled a lawn chair up to the computer and turned it on. "Do you have a password?"

"I don't think so." Evelyn moved to one side of him, Bethany to the other.

He found the browser, then typed, *"Nancy Temming."*

"I thought you said her name was Hall?" Evelyn pursed her lips.

"According to her driver's license that she had to produce to secure a booth, her real name is Temming."

The internet wasn't very fast and Bethany chewed her lower lip. Nothing came up for Nancy Temming, but when he removed the first name, a number of articles appeared.

"Click on images." As they cluttered the screen, Bethany scanned the faces. She reached the third one…and gasped.

Joshua had never seen the woman claiming to be Bethany's aunt, but the modern headshot of Nancy Temming and the 1943 image of Nan Hall looked identical.

"Click on one of the articles," Bethany urged him.

He did so. The article was from a Seattle newspaper with the headline, *All Fraud Charges Dropped.* He didn't want to take the time to read it. "May I use your printer?"

"Of course. Did you find something?" Evelyn turned the printer on.

"Yes." Joshua had no time to explain. They needed to get back on the road.

Evelyn had picked up the 1943 photo. "I feel like one of those CSI or investigator-types."

As soon as the article had printed, Joshua added the current headshot of Nancy.

Evelyn picked up the printouts, moved to the table and sat, seemingly lost in her thoughts.

Joshua used her distraction to mouth the words *We have to go* to Bethany.

She nodded her understanding.

"Alma, a couple of years ago, made a comment to me over lunch one day." Evelyn was almost speaking to herself. "She said she'd had a visitor to the museum who was a doppelgänger—a woman who looked eerily similar to another person."

"Why didn't Alma think the visitor was a descendant of the woman in the photo?" Bethany asked.

"That's what Alma originally thought. She didn't think there were any descendants and was excited to find one. She showed the visitor a photo and found out they weren't related. I didn't think anything about it at the time because Alma was always into the strange, unexplained, or mysterious."

Bethany paused in gathering the articles. "Did she give you a name?"

"No. That's why I didn't connect the dots until now." Evelyn laid the two images side by side. "Hmm. Let me find my magnifying glass." She stood and moved into the kitchen.

"Don't drag her into this," Joshua whispered to Bethany. "We've got to get moving."

Before they could leave, Evelyn returned with an oversize magnifying glass, sat down and examined both images. "This is so, so fascinating! I just wish Alma was here."

He moved away from the table toward the door. "Evelyn, I don't know how to thank you enough for all your help."

"Wait, what?" Evelyn looked back and forth between them. "That's it? That's all you needed?"

"It would be nice if you'd let us take the two photos." Bethany gave Evelyn an engaging smile. "I'll mail you back the historical one."

Evelyn pursed her lips again. "Technically it's your relative, so go ahead and take it. Promise me, though, you'll let me know what happens next."

"I promise." Bethany scooped up the photos.

A phone rang from the kitchen.

While Evelyn answered it, Bethany and Joshua took the opportunity to leave.

"Just a minute," Evelyn said into the phone. "They're still here."

Joshua jerked to a stop. No one should know where they were.

"It's Shirley, from the museum." Evelyn held out the handset.

His stomach tightening, Joshua took the phone. "Hello."

"Just so you know," the docent's starched voice blasted his ear. "I'm not your answering service."

"I—"

"Tell your older friend…"

Joshua's mind drew a blank until he remembered Bethany had dyed her hair gray and was still in her makeup. "Yes?"

"Tell her a man called. He said if she ever wanted to see her sister again, she'd better get over to her aunt's place. You got that?" She hung up without waiting for an answer.

Joshua kept holding the handset, now buzzing with a dial tone, for a few stunned seconds before returning it to Evelyn. "How would anyone know we came to your house?"

"This is a very small town." Evelyn sniffed. "If someone needed to find you, it wouldn't take much. So, was that your elusive aunt or the mysterious Nancy?"

"Something like that." He gave her a nod of goodbye, waved Bethany toward the rental truck and swiftly followed her. He didn't speak until they'd returned to the main road out of town. "We misjudged them. They're not coming after us. They're making us come to them."

Bethany found herself clutching the shoulder strap of her seat belt as if that would restrain her fears.

Joshua's calloused hand closed over hers and gently loosened her grip. He kept her hand in his and started to pray. "Lord, we sure could use Your guiding hand right now. Show us, direct us, and keep us safe, especially Ruth, dear Lord."

By the end of his whispered prayer, Bethany had calmed a bit. "Yes, dear Lord," she breathed. "Amen."

Joshua rolled the window down slightly and took a deep breath of pine-laden air. "We'll figure this out while we drive. They could do the same routine and try to block roads, but there's no way they can cover every road this far away. Just to be safe, we'll just take a few back tracks. Once we get closer to Nan's place, our options are limited, but we'll jump off that bridge when we get to it."

"Apt image."

"We'll need to wait until dark to approach the place. I wish I had all my topographical maps to figure out the best approach, but I don't think we can take the chance that they haven't stationed a goon or even booby-trapped my place."

Bethany rubbed her arms. "How long before it's dark?"

"We have a couple of hours."

She tried to relax, but she still felt twitchy. "What are your thoughts on what we learned from Evelyn?"

"Did you get a chance to really study the photos and compare them to each other?"

She laid the images side by side on her lap, her eyes darting between them, before finally looking up. "The biggest difference I can find is that Nancy's hair is slightly lighter."

"Both easy enough to change," Joshua said. "Look for something hard, if not impossible, to change without surgery."

Bethany bent over the photos again and studied them. “Ears.” She straightened. “The earlobes are different. Nan Hall had attached lobes while Nancy Temming has rounded.”

Joshua gave her a quick smile. “Good catch.” He checked the rearview mirror and asked, “What does the article say?”

Joshua’s praise lightened the weight on her shoulders for a moment. She pulled out the article. “‘Nancy Temming of Tacoma was charged with fraud for selling vitamin capsules and claiming they were miraculous weight loss pills.’” She skimmed the article and gave him a recap. “The charges were dropped when the legal copy in the package insert was shown to have a disclaimer about actual results. It also says she was earlier investigated for insurance fraud. The prosecuting attorney on the weight loss case, Robin Miller, is quoted as saying, as in every such case, all they need is definitive proof of fraud to put her away.”

“So we do have someone we can turn to, someone aware of Nancy’s past. It’s clear Nancy Temming was pretending to be Nan Hall. With her background, she could have been trying to stay under the radar from the police. There’s a couple year gap between the article and when she came to Pierce. Who knows what other types of fraud she committed where she wasn’t caught. But…”

“But why kidnap my sister and try to kill me? Why erase our existence? Where do we fit in?” Bethany watched the passing vistas of rugged, pine-covered mountains. “So,” she said slowly. “Let’s try to reason this out. We know Nancy has committed fraud, even if she was never convicted of it. She would probably be looking for her next score. Stepping into the role of Nan Hall fits, but it doesn’t get her anywhere. She’d hardly get rich living on a remote mountaintop in north central Idaho.”

“But she did make money. Remember the Carmel Edition Range Rover parked in her garage?”

Bethany took out her notebook and opened it to a clean page.

She wrote *Known* and *Unknown* on the top of the page, then drew a line between them. "We know she's drawn to committing fraud. In this case, she was pretending to be a woman over a hundred years old."

One side of Joshua's mouth twisted, as if tasting something sour. "Maybe she was just stealing the identity to get social security. A common enough fraud." He gave a short shake of his head. "That's not going to bring in the kind of money she obviously has access to with that car."

Bethany had jotted government fraud on the Unknown column. "Let's keep with knowns for a bit. We know she sells huckleberry preserves at the local festivals. She has a great deal of money, at least enough to buy that car." She wrote each point in the Known column. "We know that at least three people are working hard to get rid of me and my sister. We know…" She turned back a page and added the earlier comments. "These people are thorough, well-funded, tech savvy, calculating, cunning, ruthless. Possibly willing to kill." She stared at the page for a moment, then put a line through *possibly.*

Joshua looked over at her notes. "I think the biggest unknown would be who else is involved? And are they connected to Nancy at all?" He frowned. "They have to be connected. So what is the con?"

"What if Nancy started by simply stealing Nan's identity, but she got to thinking about what it would mean to supposedly be over a hundred years old and look like she was in her forties?"

"Can people be that gullible?" Joshua asked.

"Are you kidding? What about the earth is flat? The moon landing is a hoax? World leaders are shape-shifting reptilian aliens controlling humanity? They don't need to convince everyone. Just enough to make a huge profit."

"I see where you're going." Joshua slowed to navigate a sharp turn. "Her last bit of fraud had to do with weight loss. She sees people's weaknesses—grandiose claims of easy weight loss.

Now maybe she can claim to have the answer for staying youthful. She creates a product that people *want* to believe is true."

"Huckleberry preserves." Bethany checked off the words. "She gave Ruth and me a jar and I mentioned they had a reddish color. I found food coloring in her cupboard, so she must have changed the color of the berries. Huckleberries can't be cultivated. They're wild, hard to harvest, and completely seasonal. What if she claims she found a special type of berry? A secret patch and only she knows the location? That fits all of the first comments in the Known column." She tapped her notebook on her knee. "Then she ends up with a lot of money."

"Which could mean she sold her idea or gets an investor—someone who believes her story."

"Or maybe Nancy finds someone like herself willing to invest in defrauding the public. All is going well, she's maybe doing test marketing, and the unexpected happens."

Joshua looked at her, his intense gaze briefly making her forget what she was about to say. "Um…two unexpected things happen. Ruth and I show up. Two real relatives of Nan Hall."

"You said you had no other relatives, so you two carried the only DNA profile that could prove Nancy Temming was unrelated to the real Nan Hall. The definitive proof that prosecuting attorney needs. So, you both had to be disposed of."

Bethany looked down and checked off all the words in the Known column. "One hundred percent, that fits. But we still don't know who's behind the woman at my house and the two men who kidnapped me."

"The one thing we do know is that they'll be part of that welcoming party waiting for you at Nancy's cabin."

The last few miles as they grew closer to Nancy's place, Joshua had to concentrate on his driving. He clung to his sense of direction and memory of the layout of the land. He'd long since left paved roads, and they'd threaded their way over forest service and logging roads. Small streams crossed the dirt path, creating deep mud that threatened to bog down the pickup. Daylight was sinking behind the mountains when they reached a dead end. A large pine had fallen across the road. "We walk from here." He parked and turned off the engine.

They got out of the truck. Bethany made sure Izzy had a chance to relieve herself, poured some bottled water onto a paper towel and wiped the old-lady makeup off her face, then filled Izzy's water dish. She ushered the dog back into the truck and left the window down for fresh air.

"You know, I've always wondered why she doesn't jump out," Joshua said.

"Path of least resistance." She smiled. "She'll stay where it's comfortable. Right, girl?" She scratched the dog behind the ear.

Joshua put the truck's keys into his jogging belt, scanned the terrain to get his bearings and pointed. "Nancy's cabin should be over that ridge. We'll get as close as we can, then figure out what's going on."

She nodded.

They set off on foot, the wilderness pressing close around them. Between the truck and the ridge lay a steep-sided gulch, its walls choked with brush and tangled roots. At the bottom, a narrow stream murmured over rocks, its voice just loud enough to muffle their movement. Joshua didn't bother whispering—nature provided its own cover. They descended carefully, half walking, half sliding on the loose earth, grabbing at scrubby shrubs and twisted saplings to slow their fall. Pebbles skittered ahead of them, rattling like warning signals into the gully below.

The other side was worse—loose shale, slick pine needles. Every step forward slid two back. Joshua's breath rasped loud in his throat. Midway up, he paused, hands on his knees, sweat burning his eyes.

Bethany had stopped a few feet ahead. Dirt clung to her face like ash. She didn't speak—just leaned against a pine and wiped her face, smearing it further. She met his gaze, gave him a faint smile, turned and kept climbing.

He followed, his heart pounding. Darkness had gathered fast. Night could be their friend, but if they weren't in position, it could be their undoing.

Just before they reached the crest of the hill, Bethany crouched down. Joshua joined her. He didn't know how close they'd be to the cabin. On hands and knees, they crawled the last few feet and peered down.

The cabin was below them facing left, with the garage and barn between them and the house. On the right side, the hill-side dropped off sharply to a gully. Joshua could see no sign of anyone—the cabin looked peaceful, unchanged, dark, with no vehicles parked in front. A breeze rustled the tops of the pines, sounding like breathing. His gaze swept each building, the shadows, the surrounding trees. Sweat beaded on his forehead and trickled coldly down his back. He caught Bethany's attention and crawled backward off the crest of the ridge.

Once they were well below the sightline of the homestead, he stood, helped Bethany to her feet and leaned forward. "You need to stay here and keep watch," he whispered in Bethany's ear. "I'm going to circle around the back side of the cabin, using the outbuildings as cover. I'm going to try—"

A crackling, rustling sound came from the dense forest behind them.

Bethany turned and grabbed his arm.

Joshua instinctively reached for a gun that wasn't there, then pushed Bethany behind him.

The rustling grew louder, closer, now accompanied by a huffing sound.

Joshua's mouth dried. He looked around in the fading light for a branch, rock, anything that could be a weapon.

The huffing was almost upon them.

Bethany moved so she was standing beside him, her eyes huge.

Izzy burst from the bushes, spotted them and joyfully sprinted the last few feet.

Bethany dropped to the ground as if her legs could no longer support her. “Oh, Izzy,” she breathed, then looked at Joshua. “I’m sorry,” she whispered. “She’s never done something like that before.”

“At least she can track,” he whispered back. “The plan doesn’t change. You’ll just keep Izzy with you.” He worked at getting his breathing back to normal.

“Bethany.” Somewhere in the distance, a woman’s voice rang out. “Bethany? I know you’re out there.”

“That’s Ruth.” Bethany rolled over to her hands and knees, then crawled back to the crest of the ridge.

Joshua followed, muscles clenched. He ended up on his stomach, peering through the brush.

Backlit by the open cabin doors, a woman stood on the porch. “Bethany? Bethany! I got away. Please, Bethany, if you can hear me, I—I need to come home.” Her voice broke.

Bethany started to rise when Joshua put a restraining hand on her arm. “Wait a moment. For all she knows, they’re still out there. Why would she call from the porch?”

They stayed hidden, watching.

“Please come.” Ruth’s voice was jagged with emotion. “Please be out there.”

When Bethany turned to Joshua, he saw the anguish in her eyes. But he shook his head. “I don’t like it. It feels like...”

A man stepped out of the doorway, walked up behind Ruth, grabbed her and held something up to her head.

The cabin light glinted on the pistol in his hand.

NINE

Bethany couldn't move. Her fingers dug into the cold earth. Her vision narrowed. "H-he…he's going to kill her," she whispered. Before Joshua could stop her, she leaped to her feet and pitched forward down the hillside. Thick brush, slippery pine needles and hidden, downed logs slowed her progress, but not her resolve.

The man with the gun turned in her direction. He smiled.

She kept running. She had no clear idea of what she would do once she reached her sister, but she knew if she didn't appear, he would kill Ruth.

Before she reached the porch, he withdrew, dragging her sister by her hair. "No, Bethany—" Ruth blurted out before he flung her into the cabin.

Bethany jerked to a stop, her heart thundering in her ears so loudly she could barely hear when the gunman spoke.

"Where's your boyfriend?" The man had leveled the pistol at her.

Her mind briefly went blank. She needed to conceal Joshua's presence if he were to have any chance of rescuing them. "I…uh…the message I got was that Ruth was here and ready to be picked up. I dropped Joshua off in Orofino so he could get his truck and trailer. I told him I'd meet him after I got Ruth." *Please, please, Lord, let him believe me.*

Behind her, someone crashed through the bushes.

The man raised his pistol and aimed it at someone behind her. "Well, well, well."

Bethany was afraid to look and terrified to not look. She turned.

Izzy trotted up to her, her mouth open in a pleased doggy smile.

"S-see? It's just Izzy and me."

The man's eyes narrowed and jaw tightened. "If you're telling the truth, your boyfriend's heading into his own welcome party. Get into the cabin." He waved the gun.

She walked up the steps and across the porch, making a wide berth around the man. Once inside, she raced toward her sister. Ruth collapsed in her arms, sobbing. "I couldn't…they made me… I should never…"

"Shhh." Bethany stroked her sister's dark brown hair, now filled with tangles. "It's okay. You didn't know."

"Move over to that table." The man had entered and shut the door behind him. His charcoal-black eyes glinted in the light from a small kerosene lamp in the middle of the table.

Still holding on to Ruth, Bethany moved forward and seated Ruth, who continued to sob. Then she sat beside her sister. Izzy had followed Bethany into the cabin and seemed more concerned with sniffing around the room than the man with a gun. *Please, Lord, help Joshua to get us out of here.*

From outside came the sound of shouting and a man's yell; then gunfire split the wind-whispered silence.

Bethany leaped to her feet.

In three steps, the man reached her side and slammed her back into the chair. He raised his hand and slapped her hard across the face.

The room spun. Her eyes watered. Her teeth sliced into her lower lip. She put her hand to her burning cheek, then glared at the man.

He raised his hand to slap her again, then dropped it. "That's for lying that you were alone."

The door slammed open and Joshua appeared, blood streaming down his face.

Bethany started to rise again, but the man put his hand on her shoulder and squeezed—hard. His fingers dug into her.

She snapped her mouth shut to keep the moan of pain from coming out. She wouldn't give him the satisfaction of seeing her wince.

Joshua flew forward, shoved by whoever was behind him. His arms windmilled briefly before he slammed into the cabin floor. He remained there.

Bethany wanted to go to him, see how badly he was hurt, but the man squeezed her shoulder tighter.

Izzy walked over to Joshua and gently licked his face.

The pressure on her shoulder stopped and her captor crossed the room toward Joshua's attacker. They were the same two men who'd kidnapped her before. "No bullets, right?"

"Nope. Just gave him some encouragement to move."

"Ready, then?"

"This should do it."

Bethany tried to decipher their cryptic exchange.

In one swift move, both men left the cabin, slamming the door shut behind them.

Ruth rushed to the door. She tried to open it, but finding it locked, pounded on it. "Get back here! Let us out!"

Bethany raced to Joshua's prone body, swallowing the brick of dread in her chest. She gently turned him over.

He was breathing, though his eyes were closed.

"Joshua?"

He opened his eyes and stared at her, at first blankly, then with recognition. "Bethany."

"What did they do to you?"

He reached for the back of his head, winced, then looked at his hand, now covered in blood. "I was snaking down the ridge, working my way to the back of the cabin." He pushed himself to a seated position. "One of the goons must have been waiting for me. Whacked me in the head." He glanced at the door. "Is it…?"

Ruth was pulling and rattling the doorknob, still shrieking for them to open it.

Bethany ran from window to window, peering through the glass. It took her a moment to realize what she was looking at—plywood that had been nailed over each window. "Looks like they want us to stay put." She returned to Joshua and told him what she'd seen.

Izzy made her way to the door and sniffed under it.

Ruth had finally stopped pounding on the door and regained some control. "They arrived in a helicopter shortly after you left. They said they needed to get us out because there was a forest fire. They said you'd made it out and we'd be joining you soon." She blew her nose. "They told me their plans and told me I would soon be very rich if I'd go along with it."

"Something about Nan?"

"Right. How did you know? Who are they? What—"

Outside, some clinking sounds penetrated through the door.

Izzy barked.

They all looked toward the door. The small crack underneath now glowed.

A slender tongue of flame whispered under the door, then crept higher, snapping at the air. In seconds, it climbed the door, multiplying and spreading with terrifying speed.

Joshua's head pounded with pain as he looked at the door ablaze in licks of flame. His vision narrowed, and pulse raced. He tried to focus his scattered thoughts. "Check the windows in the rest of the cabin." He pushed himself off the floor and stumbled to the kitchen. He had to remember something—something important.

"All the windows are blocked," Bethany called from the bedroom.

"Same in the bathroom." Ruth's voice was shrill. "How could they?"

He turned on the water, then looked for something to put it in—a pot, bowl, bucket.

The kitchen had been cleaned out.

What was it he wanted to remember? *Important.*

Both women raced into the living room. "What should we do?" Ruth asked.

Something about the cabin.

Joshua splashed water on his face to snap out of his woozy state.

The room was growing hotter by the minute as the fire spread, now reaching for the ceiling. The crackling sound of the flames hungrily eating away at the dried logs grew louder. Izzy started barking at the inferno.

The cabin. The cabin was on fire. No. No. The cabin…was…

Someone—no, Bethany—tugged on his arm. "Joshua, snap out of it. We need to get out of here. We need to escape."

Escape. The word prompted his brain. "This was probably a moonshiner's cabin. There would be some kind of escape hatch—"

Both Ruth and Bethany shot from the room, followed quickly by the sound of furniture being shoved aside.

He staggered over to the rustic sofa and shoved it aside, looking for an even line in the floorboards where a trapdoor might be.

The heat and smoke drove him backward toward the bedrooms. Bethany was in the bigger of the two rooms, coughing at the smoke and frantically shoving the desk aside.

"Get down," Joshua yelled over the sound of the fire.

Bethany immediately dropped to the floor.

Ruth staggered in, coughing. "Noth…nothing. I can't fin…" Her coughing overwhelmed her.

Joshua dragged her to her knees. "Stay down. Less smoke."

Izzy began frantically barking from another room.

"Izzy!" Bethany scrambled past Joshua before he could stop her. "Izzy! Joshua, Ruth, come quickly!"

Joshua crawled on hands and knees behind Ruth, heading toward Izzy's barking. The smoke burned his eyes and clogged his throat. The heat was like a living thing pushing toward him.

Bethany was in the bathroom next to Izzy, who was barking and backing away from the door. Her hand slid across the floor, pausing when something cool puffed against it. Air. "In here." She traced a square shape in the oak floor, then moved aside to let Joshua work on it.

He felt along the edges until he found a loose piece of wood. He pulled on it and a small metal handle came up. He grabbed the handle and pulled.

A chunk of the floor lifted and a black hole appeared. There was no sign of a ladder or stairs beyond.

"I'm going down." Bethany prepared to lower herself into the yawning darkness.

"I should go." Joshua put up a hand to stop her.

"No. If you got stuck, we couldn't pull you out. I'll go, then Ruth. Then you can hand Izzy down to us." She put both her hands on the edges of the opening, then slipped down, disappearing into the inky darkness.

"Bethany?" *Please, Lord...*

"I'm okay. It's not that far. A couple of feet and the ground is pretty soft."

"Ruth, you're next."

Ruth needed no further urging. She followed Bethany.

Izzy didn't wait for Joshua to lower her. She launched herself after Ruth.

"Oomph!" Bethany said. "Are you okay, Ruth?"

"I wasn't expecting a dog to land on my head, but yes."

Crash!

A wave of scorching air blew over him as something collapsed in the living room. He thrust himself through the hole, his head rattling as his feet hit the dirt floor.

"What was that sound?" Ruth was on his left. The flickering light of the burning cabin barely penetrated the thick darkness. It smelled of dirt and mildew.

"Probably a wall collapsing." Something dropped in Joshua's hair and skittered across his scalp. He swatted at it and winced when he inadvertently brushed against his wound. "We have to move. Put your hands out and feel for a tunnel leading out of here."

Bethany yelped.

"What is it?" Joshua asked.

"Spider. I hate spiders."

Another crash from above sent a rush of hot air and smoke down on them.

"H-how long before—" Ruth asked.

Joshua moved forward and quickly found a wall of rocks. "Not long." He kept his hand on the wall and started feeling to his left. He soon encountered Bethany.

"Nothing." Her voice was tight. "No escape route."

He wrapped his arms around her. "Lord, we need You now. Deliver us from this trap—"

Izzy started barking, sounding muffled.

"Izzy is over here," Ruth called from behind them. "She found a hole."

He let go of Bethany and turned. He could see Ruth now. The fire must have reached the bathroom. The air in the tunnel had grown hot and ash was swirling around them.

Ruth was moving a bunch of lumber that had been stacked against the stone wall. An opening, waist-high, appeared.

Joshua reached her in three strides, then grabbed the wood and hurled it aside.

Before he'd completely cleared it, Ruth popped into the hole. "Izzy's in front of me. I can feel her. She's digging, but it looks like a dead end."

Joshua found it difficult to breathe. His legs threatened to give way. *No. Not like this.*

Bethany came up beside him and took his hand.

He tried to think of something to say, but his throat closed up.

More crashing echoed from above them and sparks poured into the room. The air was barely breathable. "Get down closer to the floor," he said to Bethany, then dropped to the floor. "Ruth, back out and let me work on it."

Shortly she bumped into him. "Izzy's about four to five feet in."

Joshua crawled into the small cave. His body immediately blocked the tiny bit of light. The walls scraped his shoulders; there was barely enough space to squeeze through. The raw earth around him pressed inward. The air was thin and filled with dirt, coating his mouth and throat.

He shoved down the claustrophobic panic threatening to overwhelm him. *This is our only hope. Please give me strength, dear Lord.*

He found Izzy, digging ahead and slightly right of him. She whined slightly with her efforts, as if she knew the stakes.

He reached past her and felt. She'd dug another foot through the dirt.

They were putting their chances of survival on a dog who could simply want to dig in the dirt.

But it was all they had.

He started scooping the dirt out of the way and pushing it behind him.

"Joshua?" Bethany's voice was high-pitched. "How…it's getting…" She stopped in a spasm of coughing.

He dug faster. And prayed.

Bethany had crouched in front of the small opening next to her sister. In the flickering light, Ruth's face was ghostly pale and her eyes were huge as she stared at the inferno lapping at the escape hatch.

The heat forced Bethany to her stomach, trying to find breathable air closer to the earth, but the tunnel was steadily growing hotter. "Joshua…" she tried calling him again, but another spasm of coughing took over and she gasped to breathe. *I'm going to die.* "Dear Heavenly Father." She mouthed the words. "Forgive my sins." The room grew farther away. Her vision narrowed…then went black.

The earth moved under her. Her face raked against the pebbles embedded in the dirt. Her arm hurt…because…because someone was dragging her.

Air—real, fresh air—stabbed into her lungs like needles. She rolled onto her side, coughing up blackened phlegm. The world spun as she rolled on her back and blinked through burning eyes at the red-tinged stars overhead.

Izzy wiggled in next to her. She put her arm around the dog, pulled herself to a sitting position and hugged her hero.

A moment later, Joshua backed out of an opening in the hillside, pulling Ruth behind him.

She was motionless, eyes closed.

Bethany went to her and gently shook her. "Ruth? Can you hear me? Look at me, Ruth!"

Her sister didn't respond.

Bethany, hands shaking, felt for a pulse, then put her head next to Ruth's nose and mouth, listening for breathing.

She found neither.

She pulled Ruth's head up and backward to clear her airways, pinched her nose, then gave two quick breaths into her mouth. Without hesitating, Bethany laced her fingers and planted the heels of her palms over Ruth's sternum, right between the ribs. She began compressions—hard and fast. "One, two, three—" she counted through gritted teeth. Her arms quickly began to ache, but she kept going. Thirty compressions. Then another breath.

"You don't get to leave me," she panted out. "Come back. Right now."

Another round of compressions, her hands slick with sweat and soot.

Ruth coughed. A rattling, broken sound.

Bethany froze.

Then Ruth's chest hitched.

Bethany let out a sob and cradled her, whispering, "That's it. That's my girl. You stay with me."

Joshua's arms wrapped around her and he whispered in her ear. "We have to move, Bethany. I don't know where they are."

His word were like ice water up her spine. She nodded. "How will we move Ruth?" she whispered back. "I don't know if she can walk."

Joshua wiped the sweat from his forehead, smearing the blood, dirt and ash. "I can carry her down this gully to get some distance from here, but we'll eventually need to climb up to the ridge to get to the truck."

Bethany looked up at the steep incline they'd have to navigate, then briefly closed her eyes. *I have to do this.* "Let's get going."

Working together, they were able to get Ruth up. Joshua then bent forward and pulled the barely conscious Ruth across his shoulders. He let out a quiet grunt, then turned downhill. With the dog at her heels Bethany followed him, down the narrow gulch, following a dried stream bed. The moon provided just enough light to navigate, though in the deeply shadowed areas they both stumbled over the loose rocks.

The glow from the cabin's fire grew dimmer.

Joshua finally stopped and Bethany caught up. Sweat streaked his face and dripped off his chin. He swayed slightly.

"Joshua, wait, you can't go on. You're too badly hurt."

For a moment she thought he'd argue with her. Instead he slowly lowered Ruth until she was lying on the ground, then sat next to her. Bethany's hand shook as she checked Ruth's pulse. Still there, barely. Her sister's skin was hot and streaked with soot.

Bethany sat beside Joshua and put her hand on his shoulder, offering comfort. Sweat had soaked through his light jacket. "I'll be okay in a few. Just need to catch my breath," he said.

She looked into his face. His eyes looked sunken, his skin pale and clammy under the dirt. "Joshua, there's no way you can carry Ruth up that hillside by yourself."

"We don't have a choice."

She stood. *Send me some inspiration, Lord.* She looked around for a moment, taking in all their resources. *We need another way. If we had a horse...* Her gaze drifted to Izzy. *A big dog would work.* She turned in a circle, staring at the forest closing in around them like a noose. Trees. Rocks. Branches. A small grove of aspen. The remains of a livestock fence. Pine needles. Bracken fern. Her gaze returned to the fence. It was made of poles nailed to a cedar post, long since fallen over.

Two poles. His coat. Her coat. Her shoelaces. That was it.

She moved closer. The fencepost was rotted, but some of the poles were in fair shape. She yanked two from the post, wincing at the loud shriek of protest from the nails. She brought them to where Ruth lay, pulled off her jacket, threw it on the ground.

Before she could ask, Joshua pulled off his jacket and handed it to her. "You're brilliant, Bethany Hall. A travois."

She wanted to pause and enjoy his approval, but there wasn't time. Her fingers moved on instinct—threading the poles through the sleeves and neck holes, then zipping the jackets shut. She tied one end together with her shoelaces. It wasn't pretty. It didn't have to be.

She tugged gently on the poles. The jackets sagged, but held, forming a rudimentary cradle for her sister to rest in.

Joshua pushed himself upright, but swayed.

"You're not doing this alone," she said to him. "We'll get her up to the top of the ridge together."

Joshua wasn't used to feeling this helpless. His head pounded, the world wouldn't hold still and kept swirling around him, and bile kept pushing up into his throat. He had trouble marshaling his thoughts, formulating plans, making decisions.

Once he felt reasonably steady on his feet, he helped place Ruth on the travois. She was conscious, but very weak. "I'm so sorry." She kept apologizing. "I'm so sorry. I've had nothing to eat for a couple of days. Nothing was…"

He clenched his jaw at the depraved cruelty of the men. They'd starved Ruth, then tried to burn them all alive. He'd make sure they were brought to justice.

Once Ruth was in place, he lifted one pole of the travois, Bethany the other. Ruth was slender like Bethany, but that still meant he was lifting at least fifty pounds. But so was Bethany. His admiration for her intensified.

Together they started up the steep incline. They made it only a few feet before it was clear their plan wouldn't work. Ruth kept sliding down, and the travois caught on every branch, log, rock and bush. Further, he was compromised from the blow to his head and Bethany wasn't in much better shape. He could see from her expression that she was going to give it her all, but that wouldn't be enough. "Bethany, wait. We're going to have to come up with another plan."

She placed the pole on the ground, turned and sat. "I'm listening."

He sat as well. "The shortcut idea of climbing over the ridge isn't going to work. It's too steep to get Ruth up." He could see her face in the soft moonlight. In spite of nearly burning to death and crawling through a tunnel to escape, she looked beautiful. "This gully, from what I've been able to figure out, runs roughly north to south. The truck is east of us. I think if we follow it, the dried stream bed will run into a larger creek and eventually to a logging or forest service road. Once we reach the road, I can hike over to the truck and bring it back."

Bethany slowly nodded. "Sounds good."

Clouds dappled, then obscured the moonlight. They were plunged into darkness and the temperature dipped. They weren't moving and the cold quickly chilled the sweat on his back. *Not good.* Their jackets were on the travois and they needed to be able to see. If either of them fell and twisted an ankle or worse…

Bluish moonlight reappeared.

Joshua looked up, grateful for the clearing. Till he saw more clouds were forming and moving toward the moon at a good pace.

"Houston, we have a problem," Bethany said quietly.

"Just what I was thinking. Those look like rain clouds, maybe even sleet if that temperature drop is any indication. We'd better hunker down until daylight."

"What do you want me to do?"

"We passed a small overhang back a bit where the creek dug into the hillside. We can use that as a start." Joshua rubbed his scratchy beard to help him think. "I have my book of matches, so we'll need dry tinder like twigs, grasses, bark from a fallen tree."

The moonlight faded, then grew.

"We need to work fast." Joshua stood somewhat unsteadily. "Grab the travois pole and let's move Ruth with us. Get the tinder as we go. Once we're at that overhang, we'll use the poles to make a makeshift lean-to."

"Got it. One…two…three." Bethany lifted her side at the same time as Joshua.

The overhang was farther than he remembered and the light even more intermittent. Once they reached it, Bethany scavenged for pine needles and grasses to both start the fire and lay beneath their bodies as insulation from the cold ground.

Joshua gently lifted Ruth off the travois and placed her on the makeshift bed. Izzy didn't wait for an invitation. She curled up next to the prone woman.

As a few drops of rain struck his head he left the jackets on the travois and placed the tied end against some rocks. He broke off cedar branches as fast as he could and placed them over the jackets.

The rain increased, and the moon slipped behind the clouds for what was sure to be the final time.

"Bethany?" He could barely see his hands in front of his face.

"Here." She was suddenly next to him.

"Get under the shelter. You can't afford to get wet."

He heard rustling, followed by the snapping of twigs. He followed the sound and joined her under the lean-to. The space was tight. He pulled out the matches and lit one.

Bethany had stacked a variety of branches, bark and pine cones next to Ruth, then moved some stones to create a tiny reflector wall. With the light from Joshua's match, she piled the grasses and pine needles she'd collected into the small firepit she'd created.

A few drops of rain found their way through their jacket-and-branch thatching and struck the lit match. They were plunged into darkness.

He tried to light a second match but the book of matches had gotten damp, apparently also struck by the rain.

"Joshua?" Bethany's teeth were chattering.

He tried again. And again. And again. "Matches got wet." His hands were fumbling by now.

Bethany's smooth fingers slid around his hand and lifted the matches from him. He heard several attempts. A match flared. She placed the flame into the pile of pine needles. They quickly flared to a small fire. She continued to gently feed the small fire until it was large enough to add a stick.

The rain grew more persistent and cold drips found their way through the branches, hissing when they hit the fire.

"Is there a chance of a flash flood?" Bethany asked.

"I hope not."

TEN

Bethany tried to calm the fears that threatened to overwhelm her. *What if there is a flash flood? What if a large predator finds us? What if this fire goes out?* As she ran through a list of potential disasters, she felt the temperature drop again and noticed snowflakes raining down around them through the holes in their makeshift lean-to.

Joshua had settled cross-legged next to Bethany and put his arm around her to keep her warm. Izzy decided his crossed legs formed the perfect dog bed. She curled up and made herself comfortable. Ruth was next to Bethany, curled up on her side with her head in Bethany's lap. Bethany stroked her sister's tangled hair. At least Ruth was wearing a jacket and thick socks under her boots.

Bethany reached behind Ruth, grabbed a few more branches, then added them to the fire. The meager pile she'd collected wouldn't be enough to last until morning. Her sweater helped with the cold a bit, but any breeze cut through the thinly knit fabric.

She pressed herself against Joshua, trying hard not to shiver. She felt a gentle whisper of a kiss on the top of her head.

The gesture tugged on her heart. She had never wanted to be drawn to a man again—not after Daniel. She'd been star-struck by his intelligence, his enigmatic depth, his sophistication. She'd been young and foolish. She finally heeded the warning bell going off—his lack of moral conviction—and broke up with him. He immediately became engaged to her sister, leaving her with a deep sense of betrayal.

And Joshua was probably just as morally corrupt.

I don't care.

You will when he gets arrested for poaching all those endangered species.

He can change. He can get a regular job.

You think you're going to change him? Help him see the errors of his ways? What's changed since Daniel?

She had to stop this mental argument. Think about something else.

She looked down at her sister.

"How is she doing?" Joshua asked.

"She seems to be dozing."

"Don't let her fall asleep. Try to keep her awake."

"Ruth?" Bethany gently shook her sister's shoulder.

"What? Go away." Her sister waved a hand toward Bethany.

"I'm not going away. I—I need to talk to you."

The fire crackled and popped with the slightly damp wood. The snow drifted lazily down and gathered just beyond their lean-to.

"I don't want to talk to you." Ruth sounded irritated.

Good. Being annoyed would wake her up more. "When I left Aunt Nan's house…" The name tasted like ashes in Bethany's mouth. "I need to know what happened."

"I already told you. Two men arrived in a helicopter. They said there was a forest fire and they had to evacuate us. Now leave me alone."

"Come on, grumpy-pants. I need you to fill me in. Why were we going to Nan's place?"

"You know."

"Is she always like this?" Joshua whispered in her ear.

"No. Sometimes she's really cranky," Bethany whispered back.

Ruth lifted her head slightly. "Stop talking about me behind my back."

"I'm not. I'm talking to your side. Just tell me why—"

As she expected, Ruth rallied and sat upright. She was deathly pale in the firelight. "You wanted to have…what did you call it? A sisters' retreat. A do-over."

"How did going to Nan's place make it a do-over?"

"Are you losing your mind?" Ruth squinted at Bethany.

"No. Just my memory. I was in a car accident."

Ruth's face softened. "I'm sorry."

Bethany brushed off her concern. "I'm fine, except that I can't remember some things. I need you to fill in the missing pieces."

After a moment Ruth began. "It all started on the trip to Orofino and Pierce."

"What started?"

"You really did lose your memory."

A puff of frigid wind blew through the lean-to, threatening to blow out the fire. Bethany quickly added more wood and clamped down on her jaw to keep her teeth from chattering.

Ruth moved closer to Bethany and put her hands inside her jacket to keep them warm. "You and Daniel had already broken up, but the three of us went on the trip. I think Daniel wanted to change your mind. By the end of the trip, I think he knew the answer." She was silent for a moment and Bethany noticed her eyes were growing heavy. "I think he became engaged to me to make you jealous. At least at first." Another moment. "Maybe I wanted to make you jealous as well. Anyway, he was unhappy with a lot of things, quit his job, got one in Minneapolis. He had big plans and ambitions. He was back and forth on the new job and wanted me to be a part of it." She glanced at Bethany as if to gauge her reaction. "We'd talk or text almost every day. And then… You really don't remember? I told you everything then."

"No, at least not that." Bethany prodded her sister. "Go back to when I left you before the car accident, what—"

"Are we going to die out here?" Ruth asked, her voice low and slow.

"Not if I can help it," Joshua said. "If the snow doesn't pile up, we can still walk out of here as soon as it's light enough to see."

Ruth looked like she was about to fall asleep again.

Bethany shook her sister's shoulder. "Tell me about the bundle of money you were told about."

"What?"

"When you were picked up by the men in a helicopter. You said they told you that you would soon be very rich if you went along with something. What?"

"Oh, yeah. That."

Ruth grew so silent that Bethany was about to jostle her again. "But you know it. Don't you remember? Or maybe not. I can't keep things straight right now," Ruth said. "I told you just before you left me with Aunt Nan. She's really our great-great-aunt, born in 1925. She'd discovered an unusual patch of huckleberries with anti-aging properties. They were going to develop this and I'd be in on the ground floor."

"What did you say?"

Through heavily lidded eyes, Ruth looked at Bethany. "What?"

"What did you say about the idea?"

"What do you think?"

"I think that idea made about as much sense as eating tomato soup with a fork or nailing Jell-O to a tree."

Ruth shivered. "It was all worked out. Every detail."

"But you—"

Ruth gave her a tight smile. "I never believed in the whole fountain of youth idea." Her eyes fluttered, then closed for a moment. She continued in a weaker voice. "But the potential for income if they thought they could get away with it was astounding…" Her voice faded off to almost a whisper. "The feeling was that the *possibility* of keeping old age at bay would stand. That would be…enough…to make millions."

As Joshua listened to the sisters' conversation, he couldn't stop thinking about the situation they found themselves in. The wood feeding the fire was almost gone. It was pitch-dark and snowing, so finding additional fuel would be almost impossible. Even if they could find wood, it would be wet.

Without a fire and coats, their survival looked grim.

He should have stopped earlier, spent more time making a shelter. Gathered more wood. If they perished, it would be his fault. The weight of guilt made it hard to breathe.

Stop it. Don't.

But his thoughts circled around like vultures.

"Joshua?"

Bethany's voice finally pierced through his worries.

"Are you all right?" Her voice sounded like she'd asked before.

"I…we…we need to pray."

"Not you too?" Ruth asked.

In the dim light, he could see her glaring at him. "You don't believe in all that religious stuff like Bethany, do you?"

"Yes, I do," Joshua said simply. Lowering his head, he began to pray. "Lord, You know our situation. You know how this will all end. In Your infinite wisdom, mercy and grace, please help us, guide us, direct us. As the psalmist says, if we call upon You in the day of trouble, You will deliver us. Amen."

"Amen," Bethany added.

Ruth sniffed.

Bethany put the last of the wood on the fire.

Some of Joshua's despair had been lifted by the prayer, and he clung to the glimmer of hope he'd been given.

Profound silence, occasionally interrupted by a small crack from the dying fire, settled over them. The cold, kept slightly at bay, now crept in like a fog. Bethany nestled closer. Even Izzy shivered.

Something thudded beyond their lean-to.

He would have dismissed it as just snow falling off the trees, but it came again. And again.

Bethany tensed against him. Izzy's head shot up, ears forward.

Thump. Thump. Thump.

Something was walking toward them. Something large.

"W-what's that sound?" Ruth whispered.

Thump. Thump. Thump. Creeeeek.

Then silence.

Every muscle in Joshua's body tightened. If this was a bear…

He couldn't finish the thought as the barrel of a rifle appeared inches from his head.

He didn't move.

Izzy growled.

The rifle shifted toward the dog. Then moved again and took aim at Bethany.

Joshua was about to grab the barrel when a face appeared. Otis Messick.

"Well, whatcha know about that." Otis turned his head and spit, then returned his gaze to the three of them. "You look like you're in a world o' hurt there, McGregor." He squatted down beside Joshua and stared at the two women. "Saw the cabin fire," he said in a conversational voice. "Came over to check it out. Couple of city types were hanging around, watching." His gaze took in their dying fire, too-thin clothing, the soot and blood on Joshua's head, the expression of terror on the women.

Before Joshua could ask for help, Otis disappeared.

Joshua opened his mouth to reassure the women, but no words came. He didn't want to look at Bethany, to see the fear on her face.

Something long, covered in a green plastic tarp, thudded next to him. Then the sound of thumping, growing softer. Joshua realized it was Otis's mule making the noise.

He pulled the package over and opened it. The rank odor of unwashed bodies, mule and dirt assailed his nose.

He didn't care.

Otis had left a sleeping bag wrapped in a small piece of tarp.

"Thank you, Otis, and thank You, Jesus," he whispered. He opened the sleeping bag, then unzipped it and spread it over the three of them. He tucked the tarp beside him where the wind had been sending snowflakes over his arm and leg.

No one spoke of the smell.

The fire sizzled out as they huddled under the thick covering.

"I suppose you're going to call this your God's answer to prayer." Ruth finally spoke.

"Absolutely!"

"Yes!"

Both Joshua and Bethany spoke at the same time.

Soon even the embers were gone, and they were plunged into darkness. Joshua tried to stay awake, but the warmth of the sleeping bag lulled him to sleep.

Izzy's stirring woke him. He opened his eyes to chilly sunshine. Both Bethany and Ruth were still sleeping, the pungent sleeping bag pushed away from their faces. He would have liked to stay for a bit and just watch Bethany sleep, but the pins and needles in his legs from sitting so long in the same position forced him to move.

The sisters stirred as soon as he straightened his legs.

Ruth had taken a turn for the worse during the night. Her face, if possible, had grown more pale, and her lips had a purplish cast. She started coughing as soon as she moved.

"We have to get her help as soon as possible." Bethany stroked her sister's hair.

"Do you think you can manage part of the travois?"

"Yes. We'll be going downhill."

Joshua wasn't sure his legs would hold him when he first stood, but soon circulation flooded his limbs. The cold was another matter. The snow was close to six inches deep. "We'll zip up your sister in the sleeping bag and put her on the travois. She'll be warm at least."

Working as quickly as they could, they turned the lean-to back into a travois. The jackets were frozen and stiff, but they laid the sleeping bag on them to provide warmth and comfort.

Bethany untied her shoelaces holding the narrow end of the travois, then retied them around the piece of tarp she put at the foot. "That should help us move faster over the snow."

Joshua smiled at her. "Have I told you lately that you're brilliant?"

"Define 'lately.'"

His smile broke into a grin, but it quickly faded as they maneuvered Ruth into place. She was so weak that she could barely stand. He didn't need to say anything to Bethany. He knew she was thinking the same thing.

They were in a race against time.

Bethany's back throbbed, her legs ached, and her head still pulsed with pain from the car accident. She couldn't even remember the last time she'd eaten. Add to that the strength-sapping cold, her boot without laces flapping uselessly and collecting snow, and she just wanted to curl up and have a good ol' pity-party crying jag.

And Izzy was probably hungry enough to chew on sticks.

But her sister needed her. Ruth was the only real family she had left.

Bethany took a deep breath of the frigid air, then picked up one side of the travois just as Joshua picked up his side. Wordlessly, they plowed forward through the ankle-deep snow. At least the exertion dulled the cold, but she needed a distraction from their situation. "Why did Otis help us?" She tried to keep her voice steady. "From what you've told me I thought the brothers hated everyone."

Joshua's breath hung in the air like a puff of smoke. "The Messick boys are a rough lot, that's for sure. Who knows? We did pray for help—though I doubt Otis Messick would ever think of himself as a hero." He huffed slightly, in what might have been a chuckle.

"Maybe." Bethany thought about it. "The weird thing was that Izzy didn't seem more upset about a stranger. I mean, she growled a bit, but that was it." She glanced back at where Izzy was slogging behind them, following in the trail broken by the travois. The dog would stop and grab a mouthful of snow, then catch up. "Maybe Izzy knew—" Bethany stumbled over a rock buried under the snow and almost dropped Ruth.

Joshua stopped until she could recover.

Her boot had been sliding up and down her foot and, even with her thick socks, she knew blisters had formed and broken. Her fingers were numb, stiff and clumsy. Didn't people lose fingers when they got frostbite? How would she be an artist without her fingers? *Think about something else.* "Um…can I ask you a personal question?"

"Depends." He glanced at her with the same penetrating gaze he'd given her before.

"Would you… I mean…could you ever leave the lifestyle you live?"

"What lifestyle is that?"

"You know. Poaching."

This time Joshua stumbled, then caught himself before he fell. "Let's take a slight break."

They both gently lowered the poles.

Bethany shook out her arms, then stuck her hands under her arms to warm them.

Joshua opened and closed his mouth a few times, as if to speak. He finally said, "If I told you I like what I do and I think it's important, would you trust me enough not to ask anything more?"

Now it was Bethany's turn to search for words. A part of her—a big part—wanted to lie, to preserve the growing feelings she had for him. But she couldn't lie. She finally said, "I don't know."

Joshua gave a short nod of his head, then reached for the travois. "Honest answer."

She picked up her side. The change between them was like a door quietly closing on the warmth she'd felt. Now being with him felt as cold and brittle as the day. *Fool, fool! Why did I have to ruin everything?*

Because she couldn't live with someone who would so blatantly break the law. Someone who wasn't completely honest. *That's why I broke up with Daniel.*

That thought almost made her stumble again. She'd never analyzed why she broke off the engagement. And now her tattered, unreliable memory wouldn't help her.

The sun finally appeared in their narrow gully, warming the air and melting the snow. Though Bethany wanted to bathe in the sunshine, the snow layer that had helped their passage was no longer there. The travois thumped and twisted over the uneven rocks of the stream bed. Each bump caused Ruth to groan slightly.

"Joshua," Bethany finally said. "Could we switch sides? My arm is—"

Joshua gently lowered his side. "Of course." His voice was controlled, but he didn't look at her.

Her eyes blurred and she blinked rapidly so he wouldn't see her tears. *Better now than later.* She'd probably only felt…whatever it was that she felt…because she was grateful to him for saving her life. More than once. And she was bone-tired. Emotionally drained.

And feeling empty and hollowed out.

They resumed their journey. Bethany gritted her teeth and focused on placing one foot in front of the other. Her arm burned and felt like it was being pulled from the socket. The raw, bleeding blisters on her foot made every step agony. Her mouth was cotton-dry. The dry stream bed now had water running in it from the melting snow, soaking her leather boots.

Whap! Whap! Whap!

It took a few minutes for the sound to register in Bethany's brain. The travois pole slid a few inches through her hand. Joshua had stopped and was looking up in the air.

Whap! Whap! Whap!

The sound of the helicopter grew louder.

Friend or foe? Bethany looked at Joshua. The men had abducted Ruth in a helicopter under the guise of saving her from the forest fire. Were they coming back to make sure no one escaped?

No one else even knew they were out here. Except Otis. But Otis didn't look like the kind of person who'd call in the cavalry.

"We should hide!" she screamed over the deafening sound of the rotary blades, then frantically looked for cover.

There were only a few shrubs nearby. The trees were higher up on the hillside. They'd never make it dragging Ruth's travois.

She leaned over and covered her sister with her body.

Joshua had two thoughts: If it was the men returning, they had no chance. If it was help, would they be seen in the narrow gully?

Before he could react, the helicopter passed almost overhead.

He didn't know if he should be grateful or bitter.

"Who do you think that was?" Bethany asked as soon as the noise had abated enough to be heard.

"I couldn't see if there were any markings on the side." He reached for the travois pole. "Let's keep moving. We can't spend another night out here."

Bethany picked up the other side. She winced, clenched her jaw and began moving.

It wasn't lost on him that she'd placed herself between the danger and her sister. He'd never met anyone so brave or determined. She refused to give up, even though she was exhausted, injured and undoubtedly afraid.

Why couldn't he trust her with the truth? Why did he let this gulf open between them? It was now abundantly clear he was trapped by the years of isolation, guarding his identity… And maybe even guarding his heart?

Tell her. Just open your mouth and say something.

"Bethany—"

"I think I see something." She was staring ahead and to her right.

He looked in the same direction. Between the branches of a grove of alder, something flashed blue and white.

They moved faster, but cautiously, forward.

The trees thinned out and the ground flattened. A modest white house sat in a clearing. Behind it was an old, unpainted barn. The flashes of color came from the laundry hanging on a clothesline.

A short, rather steep, incline rose between the stream bed and the homesite. "I'm going to carry Ruth from here. Help me get her onto my shoulders."

The poor woman was barely conscious. It took both of them and a lot of grunting to get her into the fireman's carry. The movement made Joshua dizzy, and he staggered a moment.

"Are you okay?"

"Climb up ahead of me. I'll be fine." He was lying through his teeth. He silently prayed for strength.

Somehow he made it with Bethany tugging on his arms. He gently laid Ruth on the edge of the lawn and Bethany stooped down to check Ruth's vital signs.

"Don't move."

Joshua looked up into the barrel of a shotgun. He tore his gaze from the black holes of the barrel to the person holding it.

A woman, probably in her fifties or early sixties, wearing weathered coveralls and an oversize brown sweater, glared at him. “Whatcha doing with those two women? What happened to her?” She waved the gun at Ruth.

“We need help.” Bethany stood, again placing herself between the older woman and her sister.

“I can see she does. You escaping from the law? We get a lot of fugitives hiding out around here.”

“No.” Joshua shook his head, then immediately regretted it. “We—”

“Stay put. I’m gonna call the sheriff. Let him sort this out.”

She started to back away.

“Wait, please.” Bethany put out her hand. “My sister needs some water, maybe something warm to drink.”

The older woman stared at Bethany, then Joshua, then moved to see Ruth more clearly. “Humph. You come with me.” She nodded at Bethany. “I’ll get ya something,” she said reluctantly.

Bethany trailed the woman to the house, disappearing behind the flapping clothes on the line.

Joshua sat beside Ruth. He’d somewhat grown accustomed to the stench from Otis’s sleeping bag, but he still made sure he was upwind of it.

Now that he was still, the sweat he’d worked up cooled in the slight breeze. The ground was wet from the melted snow and soon soaked the back of his jeans.

He didn’t care. Calling the sheriff was exactly what they needed.

Bethany returned with a thermos. She sat next to her sister, opened the thermos and poured what looked like hot tea into the lid. “Her name is Marilyn Gieszel. She’s actually very nice.” She lifted Ruth up slightly and helped her drink. Ruth took a few sips, then closed her eyes.

Bethany glanced up at him. "The sheriff should be here in an hour or so. Also an ambulance." She looked off into the distance. "Did you want to be here when the sheriff arrives? I mean, if…well—"

"Bethany…" He took a deep breath. "Look, I need to tell you something."

She looked over at him and squinted. "You don't have to say it. I think we know…well… I really appreciate all that you've done—"

"I'm not a poacher, Bethany. I'm a…was a Fish and Game undercover officer."

Her mouth remained open. A red glow crept up her cheeks. "Why are you saying this now? Why didn't you trust me?"

"I didn't trust anyone—"

"I don't believe you," she finally said. "Why would you let me think you were on the wrong side of the law? I think you'd say anything right about now to get what you want."

"No. I've been undercover for over three years, with the last fourteen months trying to catch a poaching ring. I didn't—couldn't—tell anyone."

She stared at him. "So what part of our time together was real? Was the truth?"

"Everything. Everything except what I did for a living." He wanted to reach for her, gather her in his arms, let her know he'd never deceive her again like that, but her rigid posture gave away her thoughts.

"Bethany?" Ruth's faint voice broke the frozen moment.

"Yes?" She stroked her sister's hair.

"I don't think…" Her breathing was labored. "I'm sorry. I'm so sorry. I've been such a pain—"

Bethany smiled at her. "You've always been a pain. What makes you think you were being anything different?" She looked over at Joshua. There was no anger in her eyes, but no trust either—just silence thick with everything unspoken.

ELEVEN

Bethany stared at the mountains rising in layered blue tiers overlooking the small homestead. Izzy settled next to her. Bethany didn't want to think about Joshua's revelation, but her mind kept circling back to it. She was relieved he wasn't a criminal and understood, at least at one level, why he'd kept his work a secret. But it felt too much like a lack of trust.

Then again, why should he trust *her*? She was a stranger he'd saved from the burning car. He didn't owe her anything.

Stop thinking about it.

Logically looking at the facts, she realized he'd done nothing to show he was being anything more than a compassionate and caring man helping someone in need.

The kiss. She'd felt the brush of his lips in her hair when they'd been huddled together under the lean-to. That had felt real. Did it count for something?

Daniel had seemed like the same type of thoughtful person. But she'd felt something missing, something not quite real about him. When she broke off the engagement, he'd wasted no time courting her sister.

Obviously, she hadn't broken his heart.

"Bethany."

Joshua's voice broke into her musings. She shifted her gaze from the mountains to his face, covered in dirt, soot and dried blood. Her pulse quickened even as she struggled to keep her face neutral. "Yes?"

"When the sheriff arrives, I'd like to help you get to the bottom of all that has happened. Recover your home and everything they took from you."

He didn't say he wanted to be with her, stay with her, become a part of her life—just help. Wasn't this a confirmation that he was just a soul steeped in kindness?

"That's very generous of you, Joshua. But I should be okay once Ruth gets some help." Her gaze briefly lingered on his face.

He was staring at her with the same intensity as before.

Her stomach tightened, and her heart thumped in her chest. She dragged her eyes from his face down to her sister. *Lord, please guide me.*

A faint hum grew into the roar of engines and crunching gravel. A sheriff's SUV and an ambulance pulled in front of the house.

Relief washed over Bethany so strongly she almost sank to the ground.

Marilyn strolled out and pointed toward them as Bethany waved both arms in the air.

Two EMTs jumped out of the ambulance, strolled to the back of the vehicle and pulled out a gurney.

Izzy barked at them, then cheerfully trotted over to greet them as they hurried over. While one of them bent over Ruth, the second looked at Bethany. "What happened to her?"

"She was kidnapped, held captive without food and probably without water for a couple of days, then was in a house fire."

The man didn't speak, but his eyebrows shot up. "Anything else?"

"Last night we were in a lean-to during the snowstorm, so maybe hypothermia—"

"She's tougher than my old hound dog." The man gave a short nod, knelt on the other side of her sister and quickly tossed the odorous sleeping bag aside.

Bethany stepped backward to give them space and stumbled into Joshua. He caught her before she could fall. He kept his arms around her for a moment longer than necessary before he dropped them.

The feeling of his warm, strong arms lingered, and her chest ached with wanting it back. *What have I done?* She wanted to feel him holding her again.

The sheriff's deputy had reached them by now. This was a different officer than the one she'd met earlier. "Come over to my rig and let me get some information from you." He looked closer at Joshua. "What happened to you? You have blood all over your face."

"Ambushed. Long story."

"Tom," the deputy called to one of the EMTs, "better check out this one, too." He motioned to Joshua, then turned back to Bethany. "I guess that leaves you to talk to for now. Please follow me, ma'am." He walked to his SUV and opened the back door. Izzy, who had been trailing, jumped onto the seat. "Well, okay, you have a seat too, pooch. Miss, why don't you sit here? You look a bit done in."

Bethany slid into the seat next to her dog. The SUV was still warm from the drive up. It felt wonderful.

The deputy took out a pad and a pencil. "Let's start with basics. Your name and address as well as the address of the other two."

While Bethany gave the information, Joshua followed Ruth's gurney to the ambulance. He seemed to argue with the EMT while glancing over toward her, but ultimately he stepped up into the ambulance.

Bethany worried her sweater in her hands as she watched the vehicle turn around and drive away.

"Ms. Hall?"

She realized the deputy had been trying to get her attention. "Yes?"

"Could you tell me what happened?"

She took a deep breath and started with waking up at Joshua's cabin. When she reached the part of her story where she went to the sheriff's office, he held up his hand. "Whoa there.

Let's take a break and let me call in and let them know what's happening. I'll have Ms. Gieszel make you a cup of her tea, okay?"

"That would be nice. Actually, I'd be all over that tea like a hungry kid on a cupcake."

Marilyn met them at the door. "Dog stays outside."

"Stay here, Izzy."

Izzy found a spot in the sun and flopped onto her side.

Marilyn jerked her thumb at the white-painted kitchen table and chair. "Have a seat. What's going on, Joe?"

He murmured something, smiled at her and left.

Marilyn pulled the cozy she'd placed over the simple ceramic teapot, put a chipped mug on the table, and poured a cup. "Sugar? Milk? Don't got any lemon."

"This is fine." She sipped. It felt like sandpaper had been stowed behind her eyelids. The effect of the smoke, fire and little sleep, combined with the long walk, made her droop.

A few moments later, the deputy returned with an unreadable expression. "Are you ready to go?"

She put down the tea and stood. "Thank you, Marilyn."

"Ms. Gieszel, thank you. We'll be in touch." The deputy held the door for Bethany. Once outside, he took her arm.

She looked down at his hand. "I can walk on my own."

He didn't answer, nor did he let go. He led her to the patrol car, once again opened the back door and helped her in. Izzy didn't wait for an invitation, but leaped onto the seat. Before she could ask what the problem was, he shut the door and got in. He picked up the radio and fingered the mic. "Dispatch, Unit 225, 10-76 to HQ with one 10-15 and a canine, code 4."

"Copy, Unit 225."

That didn't sound good. "Excuse me, but what did you just say?"

"I'm returning to the department with you and your dog." He started the engine and put the SUV into drive.

"I'd like to go to the hospital and see how my sister is doing."

"I'm sure you would. Do you remember meeting Deputy Green the other day and telling him a…well, let's just say a bizarre story? Well, he has some questions for you." He looked through the rearview mirror at her. "We all do."

Joshua swatted at the EMT's hand, ignoring the gurney they tried to push him onto. "I'm fine." But the ambulance's lurch down the mountain sent a wave of nausea through him. He gripped the bench, knuckles whitening, and closed his eyes. The bumpy ride stretched on, each jolt a reminder of how far he was from Bethany.

He should've told her more. Not everything—just enough to make her understand.

"Sir, you need to sit still." The EMT eyed the blood caked on Joshua's temple.

He waved them off again, his jaw tight. He hadn't lied to Bethany. But the truth about his work would be a hard pill to swallow and a huge risk on his part. His life could end with a poacher's bullet. He'd seen photos of what they did to undercover officers—bodies left in the snow, warnings carved into flesh.

It had cut him the way her eyes had searched his back at the homestead… He couldn't shake it.

He wasn't good with words. Never had been. There was no way to dress up a life built on loss and stubborn hope. If Bethany couldn't handle who he was—scars, secrets and all—better to know now, before he let himself care too much.

The ambulance hit a rut, jarring him back to the present. "How much longer?" he muttered, voice rough.

"Ten minutes," the EMT said. "Hang in there."

Joshua nodded, but his mind still on Bethany, on the words he hadn't said.

The endless drive culminated in a mass of activity at the

hospital. Ruth was whisked off while he was led to an emergency exam room. After a nurse cleaned his wound, the doctor checked him over, peered into his eyes, ran him through a series of physical tasks, asked a boatload of questions, then sent him off for a CT scan.

By the time that was completed, Joshua had seen enough of the hospital to last him for years. Before he could leave, however, a deputy found him.

"Mr. McGregor, I'm Deputy Scott. We have some questions for you."

"And I have some for you. My vehicle is still parked where I left it, so I'll need to get there somehow after we're done. And I'd like to know how Bethany Hall is doing."

"Sure. Sure. I'll drive you over to the department and send someone to pick up your vehicle. Keys?"

Joshua handed them over and gave directions to the rental truck.

Over the nurse's protest, he walked out to the parking lot and into the patrol car. They didn't speak on the short drive over to the stationhouse, and once they arrived, Joshua wasted no time in getting out and striding inside.

The deputy led him to an interview room, left, then returned.

"What's happened to Bethany?" Joshua asked as soon as the man entered.

"She's fine." Deputy Scott sat across from Joshua. "Deputy Green's taking her statement. I hear she's giving him a pretty tall tale. We're just trying to get to the bottom of it. Why don't you tell us what all happened?"

"Have you done anything to check out her story? Did you send someone to look at the burned-out cabin?"

Deputy Scott blinked a few times. "We'll get to that."

"You might get to it sooner than later. The men who kidnapped Ruth and tried to burn us alive are still out there. Here's their license plate, by the way." He recited the number. "Ada

County. Black, 2021 Ford F-250. You'll also want to locate Nancy Temming. Supposed owner of the cabin."

The deputy didn't move for a minute, then stood. "Be right back." He left.

Joshua tapped his fingers on the table. Time was slipping away. He was at the door when the deputy returned. "Relayed your info," Deputy Scott said, jerking a thumb for Joshua to sit. "Now, from the beginning."

"Fine. But then I see Bethany." Joshua recounted the past few days, keeping his cover buried.

The deputy scribbled some notes, his brow furrowed. When Joshua finished, he leaned back. "Your story matches your girlfriend's. Problem is, no record of her exists. And you? Word's out you're a poacher."

"Fine. Whatever. When you get probable cause to keep me here, you can make an arrest. For now, I need to collect Bethany and her dog and get going—"

"We're holding her until we verify her story—unless you've got something more to add."

Joshua splayed his hands on the surface of the table and breathed deeply. He could end this charade and admit that he was an undercover officer with the Fish and Game. That would blow his cover and end his career. Then again…

His last call with his boss echoed in his mind.

"Report to my office tomorrow morning at 0800. I'm assigning you to desk duties for the foreseeable future."

"And if I don't show up?"

"Then collect your pink slip when you finally do."

His boss could be just letting off steam. Probably was. They were too close to finishing this case. His being arrested would only add to his bad-guy reputation.

But if he stayed silent, Bethany would face this alone—her identity erased, her life in the hands of men who'd burned her world. Her fierce eyes, her voice, her bravery—they anchored him.

Only Ruth, the evil men, and he knew Bethany's real identity. Only he was in a position to help her.

Say nothing and save his career. Speak up and save Bethany.

The fluorescent lights overhead buzzed. The room smelled like industrial cleaner. The deputy tapped his pen on the table in the rhythm of a dripping faucet.

He looked over at the deputy and started to talk.

Bethany paced the small interview room, counting steps. Four to the wall. Turn, four back. She was hungry, tired, hurt all over, and her mind was filled with questions.

Deputy Green stepped into the room. "Have a seat."

"I'd rather have a drink of water. And a few questions answered."

Green hesitated, placed a pad of paper on the table, turned and left.

Four steps to the wall. Turn. Four steps back. She repeated the pattern several more times before Green returned with a bottle of water. He placed it on the table. "Now will you sit?"

She complied, grabbed the bottle and struggled with the cap. Her hands were brown with dirt, covered in blisters and barely functional after carrying the travois for so many miles.

He took the bottle from her, opened it, then handed it back.

The cool water soothed her raw throat. She'd never tasted anything so wonderful. She finished the bottle.

"The three of you looked pretty rough." Green took the empty bottle and tossed it into a nearby garbage can. "What happened?" He pulled out a pen and moved the pad closer to himself.

"Before I tell you, I need to know about my sister. And what's happened to Izzy, my dog? And what about Joshua?"

"I'll get to all your questions, but first I need you to answer mine."

Bethany slumped back into her chair, then launched into a recap of the events.

Green listened, his face unreadable, occasionally jotting down some notes. He didn't speak till she had finished. "So." He cleared his throat. "You're telling me two men and a woman tried to kill you by running you off the road—"

"I don't know who was driving or in the truck."

He made a note. "Kidnapped you, kidnapped your sister, took over your house and cleaned it out, tried to burn you alive, erased your existence from the internet… Erased? What did you mean by that?"

"When I first came here, you could find no driver's licenses, no social media, nothing. Like we never existed."

"I see. And you believe they're doing all this to…?"

"They're launching a wellness scam, hyping the huckleberry as a youth elixir online." Her voice cracked, thinking of what they'd done to Ruth. And poor Izzy. "I need to see my dog."

"Soon. But you say huckleberries?" Green's mouth twisted. "People aren't that gullible."

"If you put enough money into advertising, get enough people to endorse it, and threaten anyone challenging the claims, yes, people can be misled." Bethany stood. Four steps to the wall, pivot, four steps to the other wall. "And I didn't say they believed the berries had any health properties. I said they believed they could dupe people into believing it."

"Please sit down."

She sat, but rubbed her blistered hands on her pants.

Green picked up his notepad and scanned what he'd written. She couldn't read his expression. Her throat tightened, Izzy's trusting look the last time she saw her flashing through her mind. If he didn't listen, she'd lose everything. She gripped the chair, her nails biting into the wood. "Look, if you sell the lie hard enough, people—at least some people—will buy into it. Radium was peddled as a health tonic—and people suffered and died. Horribly."

Green put down the pad, eyes narrowing, then placed the pen on top. "My wife and I saw the movie *Radium Girls*."

Bethany exhaled, hope flickering. "Exactly. Lies kill."

"Yeah, but that whole radium thing was a long time ago."

"You think it stopped with snake oil and radium? False claims, deception…" She waved her hands. "Profiteering can thrive anywhere trust can be exploited."

Green frowned.

"Look, you don't have to believe me. Go check out the burned-out cabin. Ask Joshua." Her throat tightened. *Joshua.*

"Okay, okay, we will. But you haven't answered the question of *why you*? Why did they need to go to such extreme actions to get rid of *you*?"

"*And* my sister." And, she added silently, Joshua, because he helped them. "Because we were the only ones who could prove their claim false quickly through DNA."

"The berries' DNA?"

"No. Their so-called proof of their claim was Nancy Temming—acting as our hundred-year-old aunt Nan Hall. Our family line ends with Ruth and me. Getting rid of us means no family whose DNA could prove that Nancy is not who she claims to be. No contradictory evidence. Of course, a deep dive with scientific evidence would expose the fraud, but by then, they could have collected and been long gone."

Green blinked. "Be reasonable, Bethany. Do you really think someone or some corporation would resort to murder—"

"Oh, really?" Bethany shook her head. "Have you any idea how far entities have gone to exploit trust and silence anyone speaking up?" She stood. "Or the human cost?" She looked at the floor, then back at Green. "I suspect they were going to hit the ground running on this thing, make a bundle of money, then quietly slink away." She moved to the door and grabbed the knob. "Now I've told you everything. I need to find out about my sister and my dog. And Joshua."

Before she could turn the knob, someone opened the door from the other side. A deputy poked his head in. He looked beyond Bethany at Green. "Got a minute?" he asked.

"Sure." Green moved to the door. "Sit down, Bethany. We'll be right back."

"But—"

He left, shutting the door firmly behind him.

Bethany paced twice before grabbing the door, opening it and launching herself into the hallway.

Right into Joshua.

Joshua caught Bethany before she could fall, then held on to her.

She returned his embrace. "Joshua, I—"

"Later. We'll talk later. We need to get out of here."

"How? Aren't we under arrest?"

"Did the deputy say you were under arrest?"

"No."

"Then it was an investigative detention, what's called a Terry stop." He grinned at her expression. "It helps to be in law enforcement."

She stepped back and searched his face. "Do they know you're an undercover officer?"

Two deputies deep in conversation came around the corner of the hallway and continued past them, disappearing around the next corner. Voices from other areas of the department filled the silence between them.

Joshua could tell from Bethany's pale face and tight expression that she would know the significance of his answer. "At this point, I may not be anymore. But, yes, I told them."

She reached up and touched his face.

Now it was his turn to shove down the weight pressing down on his chest.

Deputies Green and Scott appeared. "Before you two go, we have one or two more questions for you."

"We need to leave as soon as possible," Joshua said. "Did someone retrieve my rental truck?"

"We're working on it," Deputy Scott said. "Things have gotten a bit busy and we're a small department. Can anyone else provide you with a ride?"

He shook his head. "My truck's at the local vet hospital. Maybe you could give us a ride over there."

"I think that could be arranged," Deputy Green said.

Bethany faced the two men. "What else do you need to know? I've told you everything."

The two deputies glanced at each other. "Look, we'll be honest with you. We don't have the staffing to keep you two safe out there until we can find the men and woman who tried to kill you and set the cabin on fire. We have a BOLO for that black truck, but we did find it had a stolen license plate. But black trucks are as common as ground squirrels. And the white van will be even harder to locate."

Bethany swayed slightly on her feet. "So you believe me. Believe us."

"We checked out enough of your story to open an investigation," Deputy Scott said. "Found the cabin. Found your car, Bethany. And we have someone checking out your house."

"Can someone make sure my sister is safe?" Bethany asked.

"Yes. We can make sure no one has access to her, but as of now, we haven't located any of the people of interest. Like I said, we can't follow you around, so we'd like for you two to stay here in protective custody until we can get a handle on this."

"Thank you for that, but right now I need to know about my dog," Bethany said.

"She was sent to the local vet hospital," Green said. "But she wasn't wearing a collar and appeared to be injured."

"What does that mean?" Joshua asked.

"Once she got there, the vet didn't have any vaccination records," Green said. "They always have to be careful, you know. Rabies. They usually either give a rabies shot or quarantine her."

"Then we'd better go spring her," Joshua said. "If I could get that ride over to the vet, I can pick up my truck and get her dog."

"Not quite." Scott shifted his weight from foot to foot. "The local vet hospital was full, so she was transferred to the animal shelter in Lewiston. She's on a five-to-seven-day hold before..."

"Before what?" Bethany's face flushed as the answer dawned on her. "She's my dog. She's hardly a stray."

Green said, "Let's just say you need to pick her up as soon as possible." He turned to a deputy behind them. "Casey, would you run Ms. Hall and Mr. McGregor over to the vet hospital?"

A uniformed officer joined them. "Sure. If you two would follow me."

As Bethany and Joshua walked past Green, he grabbed Joshua's arm. "I hope you know what you're doing." He stuffed a business card in Joshua's hand. "Cell's on the back."

They left through the back, trailed Casey to a parked patrol SUV, and got into the back seat.

Bethany shifted a few times and gave him side-glances on the way over. He could tell she wanted to ask him questions about what had happened, but didn't want to say anything in front of the officer.

They soon pulled up in front of the vet hospital, got out and waved the officer away. "Joshua, I—"

"I'll explain it all later." Joshua updated the staff, and made sure Horse was doing well. "I'll leave the trailer here and I'll be back to pick him up," he told the technician who'd followed them out.

He turned west toward Lewiston, roughly forty-five minutes away.

"Didn't you tell me that your job required you to not let anyone know who you really are?" Bethany stared at him. "For your own safety? And you now don't even know if you *have* a job?"

"Something like that." He concentrated on his driving, not wanting to meet her gaze.

"Why?"

Because I didn't want to leave you to finish this alone. Because I want to be with you more than I want to remain undercover. Why couldn't he just say it out loud? He tried out different answers, but all of them were incomplete.

The silence stretched between them.

"I guess," Bethany finally said, "I owe you an apology for not understanding, for rushing to judgment. I hope we can be… friends…after this."

He gripped the steering wheel tighter. "Friends."

A weight settled on his chest. The afternoon sunshine now seemed gray. It had seemed like the only answer—come clean about his work and keep Bethany safe from the clutches of the people after her—but what had he gained?

Lewiston, Idaho, had ten times the population of Orofino, which had hovered around three thousand souls. Traffic had picked up, giving him a reason to remain silent. They soon found the animal shelter. Bethany jumped out and rushed inside almost before he'd even put the truck into Park. He followed her in.

She was standing in front of a counter, arms rigidly at her sides, talking to a woman on the other side. He came up behind her. "But I don't understand," she was saying to the woman.

The woman shook her head. "I'm sorry. We put 'em to sleep this morning."

TWELVE

Bethany couldn't move, her body frozen. Her mind went blank. From somewhere deep inside her, a guttural scream threatened to erupt. *No. No. No. I don't accept this.* She turned and launched herself toward the door leading into the kennel area.

She heard the woman yelling at her to stop, but she just slammed through the door.

Chain-link kennels lined either side of a central hall. It smelled of disinfectant and urine. Dogs launched themselves at the gates, barking frantically, the noise echoing loudly off the cement block walls.

She ran from run to run, peering inside through blurry eyes. *It isn't possible. Please, Lord.*

Shepherd crosses, golden doodles, pit bull mixes of all kinds lunged at her as she passed. But no Izzy.

She ran faster, her breath coming in gasping sobs. She reached the last kennel. No sign of her dog.

The woman from the front had almost caught up with her, her face red, her lips pulled back into a snarl.

Bethany turned and dodged right. A narrow space between the chain-link fence and the wall led to another door. She rushed through it into a second building, this one full of smaller runs and small-to-medium-sized dogs.

And there, in the first run, was Izzy.

Bethany opened the gate, dropped to her knees and hugged the wiggling dog. The tears burned hot tracks down her face. *Thank You, Lord.*

"What are you doing? Let go of that dog!" The woman had caught up with Bethany and had grabbed her shoulder.

"And you let go of Bethany." Joshua's voice cut through the din of barking dogs.

The woman released Bethany. "You told me you had a brown-and-white pit bull with stitches. We euthanized him—"

It took Bethany a few moments to be able to speak. "I told you I had a bull terrier, not a pit bull, and a female, not a male." She swallowed the torrent of words that wanted to fly out of her mouth.

"Whatever." The woman turned away. "If you want to claim her, you'll need to pay the impound fees, daily boarding costs, and for the rabies shot. Cash, check or credit card."

Bethany didn't think she could stand. She just wanted to stay on the cold cement floor and hug her dog. Izzy seemed content to stay wrapped in Bethany's arms.

"Izzy's safe now, Bethany, but we need to get going." Joshua extended his hand and practically lifted her to her feet. He kept his arm around her as they walked with Izzy toward the front of the building.

This feels right. She leaned against him.

At the front desk, Joshua let go of her, pulled out his billfold and took out a credit card to pay the fees. He briefly peeked at the bills inside and frowned.

The clerk grabbed the card and processed it.

Bethany's stomach tightened. Joshua was again paying for her. The motel, clothing, truck rental, meals, gas, now Izzy's fees. He'd covered it all. And now he probably didn't have a job. Because of her.

She had no idea how much money he had, but she'd certainly cost him a lot. And as of right now she had no way to pay him back. She didn't even remember if she had a banking account.

They stepped outside. The sun was disappearing behind the mountains and the long, Prussian blue shadows reached into the river valley. The temperature had dipped and Bethany rubbed her arms. Her jacket was still sitting at the homesite with the travois they'd used to transport Ruth.

Joshua led her to the truck and opened the passenger door. Izzy hopped in without help, obviously eager to get away from the animal shelter. Bethany followed. "I'll start the engine and get it warm," he said.

Once he started the truck, he pivoted toward Bethany. "I don't think it's safe just yet to return to my place—at least until they catch up with those two men and woman."

"What if they never find them?" She stared out the window at the trees lining the parking lot. The words of Jeremiah floated in her mind. *...plans to give you hope and a future.* For the first time in her life, she had no idea what the future would hold. "Joshua, I can't live looking over my shoulder. Whoever these people are, we have to find them and end this."

"The sheriff's department will do everything they can—"

"I'm sure they will. But I think they're going after the pawns. The thugs they hired to do the dirty work. You said at one point that the people doing this were thorough, well-funded, tech savvy, calculating, ruthless, and possibly willing to kill. The people we've run into are certainly ruthless and willing to kill. But I don't think they have either the brains or the money."

"Like a calculating millionaire?" Joshua said slowly.

"Or a corporation being directed by a tech savvy and calculating person."

"Nancy Temming?" he asked.

"Shall we see what she's been up to?"

Joshua drove straight to the public library. The sign announced the closing in an hour. "Why don't we each take a computer?" he whispered to Bethany.

She nodded and followed him to the computer section.

People turned to stare as they passed.

Joshua ducked his head. He hadn't thought about their appearance. They both were still grimy with dirt and soot, though the ER nurse had cleaned the blood off his face and head. Bethany still wore her boot without shoelaces and her sweater was more brown than oatmeal beige. The librarian who spotted them as they passed the checkout desk looked like she wanted to stop them. He frowned at her and she looked away.

Two computers were open next to each other, though several opened up after they sat. He'd guess they'd gotten a whiff of Otis's sleeping bag stench still clinging to their clothing.

Surrounded by the hum of the fluorescent lights he sat and typed *Nancy Temming,* the name of the woman pretending to be Bethany's aunt. He found the same articles he'd read before. *Of course.* She wouldn't be going by Nancy Temming. She'd be using the name of Nan Hall. He typed her name into the computer. Nothing.

The fictional, hundred-year-old Nan Hall had yet to emerge. He drummed his fingers on the table for a moment, then tried *huckleberries*. Nothing he didn't already know.

Bethany had moved to the printer to pick up some printouts. On her way back to the computers, she looked to her right.

He followed her glance in time to see the librarian making a beeline toward them.

"Time to go," he mouthed to Bethany.

She pivoted toward the door, smiling at the librarian as she passed.

"Thank you," Joshua said to the dour woman as he caught up to Bethany and they stepped outside.

Darkness had fallen. The air was fall-cool and crisp, full of faint traffic noise. They crossed the parking lot to his pickup and got in. The confined space smelled of sweat, dog and smoke. Izzy greeted Bethany, then settled next to her, obviously contented to not be listening to the continuous barking at the animal shelter.

"It looks like our missing Nancy and fictional Nan Hall haven't emerged," he said. "How did you do?"

"I think I'm on to something." Bethany's eyes were shining in the light from a streetlamp. "I decided to look at the corporate level, a place where there'd be a lot of money. I looked up EarthKind, the Minneapolis-based company where my ex-fiancé took a job."

He felt a brief twang of jealousy. "Okay…?"

"Daniel was there. When we met up with Nan. What if he took the whole idea of the supposed health benefits of huckleberries to this corporation and sold it to them?"

"No corporation would invest in such a harebrained scheme."

"True. But what if they saw the income potential? They just had to believe they could market it successfully and make others believe it."

Joshua's mouth twisted.

She leaned forward and put her hand on his arm. "Remember this?" She handed him one of the printouts.

He scanned the page as he stopped at a red light. It appeared to be from a website. A familiar, champagne-bottle-shaped container with a black label and gold foil type angled down the page. Across the top of the webpage, in bright green ink, it announced, *Discover Vitalixir: The Elixir of Vibrant Health! Unleash Your Inner Vitality with Every Sip!*

He handed it back. "I didn't think they made this anymore."

"They don't. But listen to the hype. 'Imagine a drink so powerful it transforms your wellness from the very first drop. Vitalixir is not just a beverage—it's a revolution in health.'"

"So it cures everything from cancer to hangnails." He gave her a sheepish look. "Confession, I actually tried it. So?"

"So did I. Now read the tiny print on the bottom." She pointed.

Vitalixir is not intended to diagnose, treat, cure or prevent any disease. Consult your physician before use. EarthKind Mfrs. Minneapolis, MN.

He crumpled the paper slightly in his grip. The final piece of the puzzle. The funding.

"EarthKind. Vitalixir sold insanely well until it was finally debunked." She let go of his arm. "As far as I know, they haven't come up with a snake-oil compound since then."

He felt her warm hand resting there, even after she let go. "That makes a twisted kind of sense." He thought for a moment. "And someone would probably go to great lengths to protect their next moneymaker."

"Like kidnapping, arson and murder?"

"At the corporate level? I don't think so. They'd need plausible deniability. I was thinking more about protecting the huckleberries from forest fire. Remember the helicopters? That ranger who was shocked at how fast they went up to douse the fire?"

A police siren in the distance filled the sudden silence.

"But then what about the rest of it?" Bethany asked. "The kidnapping—"

"Sounds personal."

She hugged her dog. "And evil," she whispered. "But this fits all the evidence."

He scratched his beard. "Circumstantial at best, at this point. No connection to the men who tried to kill us, no connection to your supposed 'aunt.'"

"But I thought the deputies believed us." Her eyebrows drew together.

"We've convinced them of the attacks, kidnapping, arson. Not that there's a big, bad, multimillion-dollar corporation behind all of this."

"They can't get away with it." Bethany's jaw tightened. "What do you think about this?" She handed him the second sheet of paper, this time a press release. "They're having a big reception and corporate announcement tomorrow evening. Lots of people. Lots of media."

"In Minneapolis?"

"Spokane."

"Are you thinking…"

"Right now they think we're dead, Joshua. What do you say we crash their party?"

Bethany smiled, then giggled, then bent over laughing. She tried to stop, but every time she did, another glance at Joshua's perplexed expression set her off again.

"Bethany? Are you all right?"

She wiped the tears off her face. Her stomach hurt from laughing. "I'm just thinking of the two of us going to the reception looking like this. I mean…just look at us. We look like two homeless people and smell like Otis's sleeping bag." She reached down and pulled off her laceless boots, exposing her torn socks bloodied by rubbed-raw blisters. She meant for the sight to be funny, but it instantly stopped her laughter.

"I suspect a shower, change of clothing and a good night's sleep will change all that."

Now it was her turn to give him a perplexed look. "How…"

"I still have the safe house in Orofino. We can regroup there."

"Brilliant idea."

Despite wanting to talk to Joshua during the drive to Orofino, Bethany fell asleep, not waking until Joshua gently shook her shoulder. "Wake up, sleepyhead."

He'd parked in the garage. He helped her from the truck, then eased Izzy out.

Bethany couldn't decide if she was more hungry or tired. She settled on hungry. "I'm—"

"Starving," he finished for her. "I'll check the freezer."

"Is there some way we can find out how Ruth is doing?"

"We'll try tomorrow."

Under the kitchen light, Joshua's skin was pale, and purple hollows had appeared under his eyes.

"Why don't you sit down and let me cook."

He didn't argue. He moved into the living room and sat in a recliner.

The freezer proved to be well stocked, as did the cupboards. She removed a frozen chicken breast and placed it in a hot water bath to thaw. The freezer also yielded frozen vegetables and garlic bread. She found olive oil, a variety of spices, a package of penne pasta, a can of cream of chicken soup.

By the time she'd cooked and combined all the ingredients and set the table, snoring came from the living room.

She moved over to where Joshua was sprawled in the recliner and watched him sleep. His dark hair lay ruffled, and his beard now completely covered his scar. She reached over and stroked his hair off his forehead.

He caught her hand, his eyes opened, and he kissed her palm.

Bethany froze, her breath catching as her eyes met his.

His gaze, heavy with fatigue, held an intensity she hadn't seen there before. Before she could question it, a car, its muffler in need of repair, roared past the house. Izzy raced to the door, barking. And the moment was broken.

"Quiet, Izzy." Bethany glanced at the blackout curtains. She stepped backward away from Joshua. "I—I came in here to tell you your dinner is ready." She strolled to the kitchen before she could say anything more.

We're friends. Right?

But he was more than that. He was her anchor against the people who wanted to kill her. Not just safety. She wanted his low voice in quiet moments, his hand brushing hers—not as a comrade in this fight, but as something deeper. The thought terrified her, yet it burned brighter than her fear of the danger outside.

She'd already filled Izzy's bowl with pasta and chicken. The dog sucked it down like a vacuum cleaner and was now staring at it as if another helping might appear.

Joshua sat at the table and looked at his dinner. "You did all this with what I had here?"

"You had quite a bit. You might want to taste it before being impressed." She sat opposite him.

He reached across the table and took her hands in his, then bowed his head. "Thank You, Lord, for Your love, grace and mercy, for seeing us through this time. Thank You for the hands that prepared this meal. In Jesus's name, Amen." He let go, scooped up a bite and tasted. "Amazing." He managed to clean his plate before Bethany had gotten halfway through.

"Coffee?" She started to rise but he put up his hand. "No, thanks. I think we should get some sleep," he said. "Tomorrow we have a lot to do."

She sank back into her seat. The kitchen light buzzed faintly, casting stark shadows across the table cluttered with empty plates and the remnants of garlic bread.

"The guest room is through there." Joshua nodded toward a door.

"Thank you. I'll just tidy up." She stood to collect the dishes, and he did, too.

As they washed dishes side by side, the clink of plates and running water filled the silence. Bethany's shoulder brushed Joshua's, and she felt the echo of his palm kiss—a moment now buried under the roar of that passing car and her own retreat to the kitchen. *Friends, right?* The question still lingered, unanswered.

"I need to take Izzy out for one final time," she said after the last dish was dried.

"Okay. I have it so no light ever comes from the house, so once you're in the mudroom, shut off the light before opening the outside door."

Bethany shivered slightly. This was what his life was like?

Having to be so careful? Maintaining a safe house? Expecting to have his home in the mountains searched? And hoping a bullet wasn't waiting for him should he make a single mistake?

She expected to spend time outside while Izzy inspected every fallen leaf, but the dog seemed to be even more tired, if possible, than she was. When they both returned to the house, she trotted over to the sofa, jumped up, and was quickly snoring.

Joshua was waiting by the door to lock it. "Sleep tight." He looked like he wanted to say something more, but instead turned and disappeared into another room.

Bethany entered the guest room—essentially an office with a sleeper sofa. Joshua had made up the bed and left a set of striped pajamas and a robe.

She really should shower before going to sleep, but the effort seemed monumental. She'd wash tomorrow.

It seemed as if she'd barely shut her eyes when she heard the tapping of Izzy's nails on the floor and water running in the kitchen. She staggered out of bed, following the rich aroma of fresh coffee and something delicious baking in the oven. "Now that's the type of smells I'd like to wake up to every morning—" She snapped her mouth shut. *Idiot.*

"I'm sure that can be arranged," Joshua said softly, then placed a mug of fresh brew in her hand.

She sat, face flaming, and tried to act calm, but inside, her heart was racing. She sipped the coffee to cover her embarrassment.

He pulled a pan of cinnamon rolls from the oven and placed it on a trivet to cool slightly, grabbed his mug and joined her at the table. "Let's go over today's plan. We'll check up on Ruth first."

She nodded.

"You're assuming this reception and announcement have to do with the huckleberry scam?"

"Yes. If it isn't, we'll just slink off and find another way to get to Nancy and Daniel. Confront the beast and cut off its head in a manner of speaking. Get them to call off their goon squad."

"Okay. So how are we going to go about this? Maybe go as media? Catering staff? Try to blend in as guests?"

"Media probably need credentials." Bethany stood, refilled her coffee cup, then returned to her seat. "Guests may need an invitation. I think catering staff is the best idea. Less scrutiny, easier to snoop around."

"Agreed. Catering staff don't get asked too many questions." He stood, gathering the plates.

"I can do the dishes—"

"I got this. Why don't you shower." He grinned at her, his white teeth contrasting against his beard.

She grinned back. "Are you implying I still smell of Otis's sleeping bag?"

"Let me put it this way. Izzy is getting ready to roll over you like a particularly fragrant patch of roadkill."

This time she laughed. "Now tell me what you *really* think."

He grew serious. "I will. When you're ready."

Joshua straightened the kitchen, keeping busy to prevent his mind from thinking about Bethany. She may never be ready to hear what he thought, how he felt. She thought of him as a friend. He didn't want to just be her friend. He'd finally come to that conclusion.

It wasn't as if he had a lot to offer her right now. He wasn't even sure he had a job. He shook his head to try and clear his thoughts.

Earlier he'd gone through the few clothes he kept at the safe house to find her something to wear. All he could find was a set of gray sweats with a drawstring waistband and a T-shirt from the local high school. They'd swing by a store in Spokane to find outfits that would pass for catering staff. Probably a white shirt and black pants.

Bethany entered the kitchen, her hair still wet from her shower, wearing the clothes he'd placed on her sofa sleeper while she was in the bathroom.

He bit the inside of his mouth to keep from laughing.

The pants bagged around her ankles and the T-shirt hung almost to her knees. "I'm ready for the red carpet." She pirouetted, then walked in an exaggerated runway style.

"You look… There are no words."

"That good, huh?" She smiled, but it didn't quite reach her eyes. "So… you ready to get started? We need to retrieve the photos and notes from the rental truck up in the mountains. If I'm right and this is the grand announcement of their new super health product, both Daniel and Nancy should be at the gala. And I should have the proof with me."

He grabbed the keys. "We need to get going. We'll fine-tune the plans as I drive."

Once on the road and heading toward the parked rental truck, Joshua kept alert looking for the black pickup. The thugs may believe they'd murdered the three of them in the cabin fire, but if they were still in town and spotted the two of them, they'd quickly be in the crosshairs.

"Bethany, there is a chance that someone would recognize you, even with your hair colored gray?"

"The same goes for you. At least your beard has grown in quite full."

They reached the rental and he put his truck into Park. "We need to bring both rigs out of the mountains. I'll drive the rental and you can drive my truck, assuming you remember how."

"Ha. I remember how to drive a stick shift. I just don't have a driver's license."

"I doubt we'll run into any law enforcement around here. We'll park my truck in the garage and use the rental to go to Spokane." He got out and Bethany slid over behind the wheel.

The rental truck's engine sputtered but caught, and Joshua

eased it onto the mountain road. Beside him were the photos of Nan Hall and Nancy Temming along with the notes Bethany had written.

After sorting out the vehicles in Orofino, they swung by the hospital. Bethany stopped at the information desk. "My sister, Ruth Hall, is here. Could you direct me to her room?"

The elderly woman behind the desk typed the name into the computer, then frowned at the screen. "It looks like she's no longer here."

"What do you mean?"

"She's not here any longer. You might try the nurses' station."

A woman in scrubs working on charts at the nurses' station looked up as they approached. Bethany repeated her question.

"She left," the nurse said. "Said she didn't feel safe here. Left against doctor's orders."

"Where did she go?" Bethany asked. "She didn't have a car or—"

"There was a sheriff's deputy here guarding her. I suspect he took her wherever she asked."

Joshua nodded. "Come on, Bethany. We need to get going. Your sister must have asked them to put her in protective custody, which is smart on her part."

In Spokane, they hit a department store, grabbing white shirts, black pants and a cheap pair of nonprescription glasses for Joshua to complete his catering-staff disguise.

Bethany added a box of Band-Aids and ointment for her blistered feet, then found soft black slippers that would pass for shoes.

The gala was at the historic and brilliantly restored Davenport Hotel. Joshua and Bethany slipped in through the service entrance and peered into the ballroom. Women in glittery gowns, men in tuxedos, and media packed the room. Joshua tried to find Nancy in the crowd, but there were too many people. He moved to the side to see if Bethany would have more success. She stared at the crowd for a few moments before shaking her head.

A small stage had been set up at one end of the room with a large projection screen behind it. Bethany stared at the screen for a moment. "Joshua, I have an idea."

"I hope it's a good one."

"I do, too. Why don't you get out there and look for Nancy. I'll join you as fast as I can."

He left her and moved to the chaotic kitchen, perfect for blending in, and was immediately handed trays of hors d'oeuvres. He looked around for Bethany, but he'd lost sight of her.

People were apparently hungry and his tray emptied before he'd made it part way around the room. Before he could decide whether to go back for more food or try to find Bethany, someone grabbed his arm.

"I don't pay you to walk around with an empty tray." A man in a suit with a gold name tag jerked his head toward the kitchen.

Joshua scanned the room quickly to see if Bethany had entered, but she wasn't in sight.

He strolled to the kitchen, grabbed a filled tray and headed back to the ballroom. Everyone was finding a seat.

Joshua's hands became slippery with sweat.

Once the room was seated, he would be exposed.

THIRTEEN

Bethany found a clipboard with the maintenance schedule for the ballroom, held it in front of her and slipped into a corner of the ballroom. Pipe and drape curtains had formed temporary partitions on either side of the small stage. A table held glossy brochures with the word LifeForce in big letters. Under that it said, 'Spark boundless energy and zest for life and unlock the secret to a longer, healthier existence!'

Her lips twisted. She dropped the brochure and stepped back.

As voices reached her from the other side of the curtain, she found what she was looking for—a laptop computer. Already attached to it was the HDMI adapter and presentation clicker. She checked the podium for a computer already set up. Nothing. In less than a couple moments she used the camera function, snapping a photo of the images from Pierce, then uploaded the photo into the program.

"Just what do you think you're doing?" A woman's voice came from behind her.

Bethany picked up the clipboard, made a show of checking something off, then looked up. She steeled her face so it didn't betray her nerves. "Last-minute checks on all AV equipment and connections," she said in her most professional voice. "Sometimes folks don't remember to bring the USB-C-to-HDMI adapter for their iPad." She moved past the woman, afraid to see if her story was accepted.

The woman didn't try to stop her.

Bethany put down the clipboard and leaned against the wall. Her legs felt like cooked pasta.

Daniel strolled past her, scooped up the laptop, and headed for the stage.

She froze.

All he had to do was turn his head and he'd see her.

As soon as he was out of sight, she moved in the opposite direction and slipped into a shadowed corner of the ballroom where the pipe and drape curtains flanked the stage's left side, partially hiding her.

"If you all would please have a seat." Daniel's voice boomed out from the small stage.

Bethany stiffened, knowing soon only the waitstaff would be standing and easily spotted.

The lights dimmed and a giant screen behind Daniel lit up with the company logo.

Bethany slid behind a decorative column and potted plants, from where she could easily see the stage.

"Ladies and gentlemen, tonight we unveil a new era of health and vitality!" The screen shifted behind him with the word Life-Force. The crowd cheered.

Daniel waited until the clapping stopped. "We are thrilled to announce LifeForce Energy Drink, a secret formula derived from Vaccinium eterniflorum, a rare berry that ignites boundless energy and restores youthful vigor." The screen changed, now showing the mountains near Nan's cabin. He continued to hype the crowd, talking about the unusual properties of the drink. "But don't just let me talk about it. You have to see this to believe it." He motioned to his left. "Now I want you all to meet someone."

Nancy walked across the stage, joining him next to the podium.

"This is Nan Hall." The screen changed and a photo of the real Nan Hall appeared. "She's the daughter of Elias and Ann MacPherson Hall." He paused for emphasis, then leaned into the microphone and whispered, "Born in 1925."

The crowd murmured, some shaking their heads while others pointed at the screen.

Bethany, in spite of herself, was mesmerized. She had no inkling Daniel could be so persuasive. Or so repulsive.

"Nan, when she was just a child, found the patch of berries and began eating them." He went on to describe the wonders of the fruit.

Bethany gazed over the crowd, trying to gauge their reaction, but they were riveted on the stage, looking at the image on the screen, then at Nancy.

Across the room she spotted Joshua. He was staring intently at something to her left. She followed his gaze.

Moving toward the stage was a woman in a sleek black gown, holding a gold clutch purse. Her hair was twisted into a knot at the back of her head and a satin-trimmed chiffon evening wrap floated around her. Something about the way she walked felt familiar. Before she could place it, the woman turned.

Bethany froze.

Ruth.

Daniel and Nancy were slightly turned toward the screen, so they didn't see Ruth approach.

Bethany made her way up the side of the ballroom, toward her sister. But Ruth reached the stage first and went up the stairs. Once there she reached into her clutch and pulled out a small pistol.

Gasps rippled through the crowd. Daniel spun, and his smile vanished. Nancy's face went pale. They backed toward the screen.

"You thought you could burn me alive, Daniel?" Ruth's voice was raw, venomous. "My own husband, plotting with *her*—" she jabbed the gun toward Nancy "—to kill me and take everything."

The room erupted in chaos. Some people raced for the exits.

Others ducked, while some pulled out their cell phones and began recording.

Bethany jerked to a stop, her mind reeling. Ruth hadn't broken up with Daniel, she'd married him. She was in on this.

Was this what she'd meant when she said she'd told Bethany everything?

Ruth crossed the stage, keeping the pistol aimed at the couple, until she'd reached the podium.

Daniel and Nancy now had their backs to Bethany.

Ruth's voice could be heard through the PA system. "This was *my* plan. *My* idea. I was the one who saw the potential with the photos. I told you about Nan and Nancy. And you tried to kill me by burning me alive." She gulped back a sob and the gun wavered.

Bethany shot forward and jumped in between Ruth and Daniel. "Ruth." She put out her hand. "This isn't the way. The sheriff knows about the people they hired to kill us. They'll take care of it—"

"Get out of the way, Bethany." Ruth's gaze locked onto her sister.

"No, Ruth. I can't let you ruin your life over these two." Out of the corner of her eye, she spotted Joshua carefully working his way to the stage behind Ruth.

"You always got everything. The men. The big breaks." Ruth's eyes were sparkling with unshed tears. "But this time I'll get it all. I told Daniel we just had to get rid of any other evidence. We just had to get rid of you." She raised her pistol again, this time aiming at Bethany's heart.

Joshua launched himself at Ruth, tackling her to the floor.

The gun fired.

"Security! Get security. Ladies and gentlemen, please, please!" Daniel tried to soothe the crowd. "Everything is under control. The police are on their way."

After tackling Ruth, Joshua picked up her handgun and put it in his pocket. He pulled her up to her feet, and keeping hold of her arm, ran to Bethany.

Blood was dripping from a wound in her arm. Her face was stark white, her eyes wide and staring.

His breath hitched, chest heaved, and he lurched forward. "Bethany!" he rasped.

She shook her head. "Stay with Ruth," she mouthed.

Daniel continued trying to calm the audience. He turned off the podium microphone, turned on his lapel mic and moved to the front of the stage—drawing attention away from the action upstage. "Let the good folks get a good look at you, Nan." He waved Nancy over so she stood next to him. A spotlight lit her up. "You'll also get a chance to meet her later."

Two men, dressed in all black with the word *Security* embroidered in gold on their pockets, jumped up on the stage.

"Get them out of here," Daniel hissed at the men.

Joshua recognized them immediately—the men who'd tried to kill them and kidnapped Bethany. Before he could move, one of the men grabbed Bethany's good arm, ignoring her wince, then looked straight at Joshua and made sure he saw the pistol he pressed against Bethany's side. He then said, "Don't move."

Joshua froze. The second man grabbed Ruth and handcuffed her, then moved to Joshua. "Put your hands behind your back," he whispered through gritted teeth.

Joshua glanced down.

Seeing a Glock digging into his ribs, Joshua complied. The man reached into Joshua's pocket, removed Ruth's gun and cuffed him.

"See, folks?" Daniel continued to talk in a soothing voice. "Nothing to worry about. This is my private security. They'll hold these people until the police arrive."

Hiding his weapon, the gunman next to Joshua grabbed both him and Ruth and started walking them off the stage.

"Let me continue with the presentation." Daniel aimed his remote at the laptop sitting on the podium and advanced the PowerPoint to the next slide. He kept his focus on the audience, moving slightly to keep them distracted and engaged. "As you can see, the main ingredient in this drink is Vaccinium eterniflorum, a rare variant of the huckleberry—"

Some of the audience gasped. Others turned their phones to the screen. Soon, murmurs turned to uproar.

"—what's going on here—"

"—who's that—"

"—I don't believe—"

Joshua stopped, halting the security guard trying to hustle him off the stage, and stared at the screen. It was the printout showing Nancy Temming's sleek headshot with the headlines from the Seattle newspaper stating All Fraud Charges Dropped. Next to it was a photo of the real Nan Hall.

Daniel turned to look at the slide. The remote dropped from his hand and shattered on the stage. His eyes widened and he turned to Nancy.

Nancy put her hand over her mouth while her face drained of color.

The audience grew louder, peppering Daniel with questions. The media rushed to the front of the stage, vying for the best views. Daniel tried to calm them, but sweat had beaded on his forehead and his complexion had grayed.

One of the pipe and drape curtains tumbled backward. Chairs clattered and several glasses shattered on the floor.

Bethany jerked her arm free and dashed to the podium. She grabbed the microphone off the stand and turned it on. "Life-Force is a fraud. Daniel Adams and Nancy Temming are both frauds." She pointed at Nancy. "I can prove she isn't related to the Hall family."

The security guard reached Bethany and grabbed her injured arm.

She screamed in pain.

Daniel jumped off the stage and attempted to run through the crowd. Outraged audience members blocked his escape.

Joshua jerked away from the gunman holding his arm and ran toward the podium. With his hands cuffed behind his back, all he could do was slam sideways into the stomach of the man holding Bethany. They slammed into the floor, Joshua on top.

Strong hands lifted him off the security guard. He was about to struggle when he saw who had him—a uniformed officer from the Spokane Police Department.

Daniel's goon tried to flee, but another officer caught him and brought him down again.

Joshua looked around for Bethany and spotted her being escorted by yet another officer—hopefully toward a waiting ambulance.

"What's going on here?" The officer's badge said *Thompson*.

"You'll want to be sure to arrest Daniel Adams, Nancy Temming and those two supposed security guards." He drew a deep breath, then continued. "I'm Officer Joshua McGregor, an undercover investigator with the Idaho Department of Fish and Game. The injured woman is Bethany Hall. I'd like to give my statement and present evidence of attempted murder, arson, kidnapping, fraud and theft."

Officer Thompson's eyebrows shot up. "Well, well, well. Looks like we're in for a long night."

Between the shot she got for pain and her exhaustion from the past few days, Bethany could hardly keep her eyes open. She was grateful for the doctors who had removed the bullet and stitched her up, and now she just wanted to sleep. But the detective standing beside her was intent on asking her questions. Having trouble concentrating, she stumbled through her explanation of the events of the past few days.

The detective stopped taking notes and looked at her. "Ms.

Hall, um…we can get your statement, at least a clearer version, after you've had a chance to rest. I can come back in the morning."

"I'm not staying here."

"Is there somewhere I can take you?"

She thought for a minute. "Not really. Wherever Joshua is, I guess."

"We're taking care of him, don't worry. Okay, I'm going to take you to a hotel for the night. I'll be back in the morning to take your statement. Okay?"

The rest of the night was a blur. She fell asleep on top of the bed and didn't wake until someone banged on her door. It was the same detective, now holding a paper cup of coffee and a sack from a bagel shop.

They sat around the small table in the plain hotel room while she ate. After she'd finished the last of her bagel, she leaned back in the stiff hotel chair, her bandaged arm throbbing faintly under the painkillers' dulling effect. The detective—his name, she vaguely recalled, was Hargrove—watched her with a mix of patience and scrutiny, his notebook open on the table.

"We've had a chance to interview Joshua McGregor," he said. "Daniel Adams and Nancy Temming, too. We've also spoken to Pete Perez and Edward Butler—"

"Who?"

"The two men dressed as security guards. They pretty much fell over themselves unloading on Daniel and Nancy."

"What about the woman who was in my house?"

"Julia Shaw." Hargrove flipped a page in his notebook. "She's the last loose end. We've got her description out, and a few leads from Perez and Butler. We'll have her soon enough. We're working together with the different departments on this."

Bethany's gaze drifted to the window, where pale morning light filtered through the cheap curtains. She hadn't had time to think that her home—her sanctuary—had been violated, her belongings pawed through, loaded up and stolen. The thought of Julia, a stranger, walking through her rooms, touching her things, made her skin crawl. "What about everything they stole?"

"I don't know about that."

Bethany didn't want to ask, but she had to know. "And my sister?"

Hargrove shifted in his seat, his expression softening but still guarded.

Bethany's grip tightened on her coffee cup. Not good.

"Ruth's been admitted for psychiatric observation."

"What does that mean, exactly?"

"She's at City Hospital, in their psychiatric ward. From what I've been told, she's not…entirely lucid. The doctors are evaluating her—trying to figure out what's going on, mentally and physically. She's not in any condition to be questioned yet."

Bethany's chest tightened. Ruth's face flashed in her mind—not the wild, desperate woman she'd seen waving the gun last night, but the sister she'd grown up with. The one who'd clung to her when their parents died, shared secret late-night talks, and laughed with her until they cried over stupid jokes. That Ruth felt like a ghost now, buried under whatever had driven her to this point.

"And… Joshua?" The bagel sat heavily in Bethany's stomach, and the coffee, though warm, did little to clear the remaining fog in her head. "So…is he okay?"

Hargrove gave a small nod. "He's fine. Shaken up, like you. He gave us his statement and put us in contact with the Clearwater County Sheriff's Office. Very helpful."

"So…you're done with him? He's no longer at the department?"

"Yes, I believe so. I think they finished with him last night."

"And…so…where is he?"

"I don't know. He probably went home."

"But…but does he know where I am?"

"I'm sure they told him where you are."

Why wasn't he here? If for no other reason than to drop off Izzy. *Fool. You told him you just wanted to be friends.* A giant brick of a lump formed in her throat.

"Now, Ms. Hall…" Hargrove broke into her gray thoughts. "I need to go over your statement again, now that you're a bit more rested. Can you walk me through what happened, starting from when you were in the accident?"

Bethany took a deep breath, steadying herself. She didn't want to start crying. Not now. She'd have a lifetime to mourn all that could have been.

Hargrove scribbled notes, occasionally nodding or asking for clarification. When she finished, he leaned back, studying her. "You've been through a lot. Most people would've cracked under that kind of pressure."

"I don't feel like I held it together." *I feel like my world has crumbled under my foolish words.*

"You're here," he said simply. "That's enough." He stood. "I'll type this up." He held up his notes. "And have you sign your statement. Then I can arrange to have you taken home." He placed his card on the table. "Here's my number if you think of anything else and you need to get in touch with me." He left.

Bethany stared at the bland hotel room, her mind a blank. She knew she needed to make plans, work on getting replacement identification, a car… *Joshua. Joshua.* Thoughts of him crowded into her mind and she couldn't think.

She finally crawled into bed, not caring if her arm bled through the bandage and smeared the sheets. She closed her eyes.

The sound of someone knocking at the door woke her and she sat up with a jerk. Looking at the clock, she realized she'd been asleep for hours. She jumped unsteadily to her feet and rushed to the door, hoping, praying it was Joshua.

Instead, a young uniformed officer stood there, holding up a Burger King bag. He took a step back when he looked at her. "Um… Ms. Hall? Detective Hargrove had me pick this up for you." He shoved the bag and an ice-filled container of soda into her hand. "Okay. See ya."

She closed the door, put the food and drink on the table, then went into the bathroom to see what had startled him. Her reflection showed her dyed gray hair in a tangled knot on top of her head, a red nose and purple circles under her bloodshot eyes.

She washed her face in cold water, then walked over and sat at the table. The aroma of hamburger and French fries made her ill. She picked up the bag, put it outside the door, then curled up on the bed holding the pillow in her arms. "Dear God," she whispered. "I need You…" Her throat closed and she couldn't finish.

Joshua waited while Izzy finished inspecting an apparently riveting blade of grass in the dog exercise area of the small park. "Come on, Izzy. Let's go."

The chunky dog gave him an open-mouthed grin and jumped in the Jeep without help. She seemed to have completely recovered from her bullet wound and brush with a fiery death. Joshua hoped Bethany had bounced back as fast.

He drove to the hotel, but when he reached Bethany's hotel room, his knuckles hovered over the door. He wasn't as confident as Izzy, who waited beside him, her tail thumping against the worn carpet.

The past few hours had been a blur. It had seemed like an eternity in the interview room at the police department. Then came the mass of phone calls, returning the rental truck, and picking up his Jeep. He still had a lot to do. The whole time he'd wanted to call Bethany, to explain. But every time he reached for the phone, he'd stopped. *What if she doesn't want to hear from me? What if she meant what she said about just being friends?* At least he could act like a friend and make sure she was safe and had her dog.

He knocked, the sound sharper than he'd intended. Izzy's ears perked up.

In a few moments the door opened, and there she was. Bethany's eyes, red-rimmed and shadowed, went straight to Izzy. "Izzy!" she gasped, dropping to her knees and pulling the dog into a hug.

His heart twisted at the sight—her gray hair a tangled mess, her face pale and drawn, but still her, still the woman who'd gotten under his skin in ways he never would have believed.

She hadn't noticed him yet, and for a second, he just watched her. Then she looked up, and her expression shifted—confusion, hope, maybe even hurt. "Joshua?" Her voice was soft. "I… I thought you were gone. Hargrove said you went home."

"I had some things to take care of."

She stood and moved into the room, Izzy close to her leg.

He stepped inside and let the door close behind him. "I didn't mean to leave you wondering."

She sat at a small table. "Well, thank you for bringing Izzy back."

"My pleasure." He sat on the unmade bed.

She looked smaller and very fragile with her bandaged arm bearing rust-colored bloodstains. She looked up from petting her dog and caught him staring at her. Her hand went self-consciously to her hair. "I'm sorry. I look a fright."

"You look beautiful."

Her fingers froze and a red flush rushed up her neck and onto her face. "You're only saying that because you've been staring at Izzy too long." She cleared her throat. "You'll be heading back to your ranch, or wherever it is you live, I guess."

"I own the ranch."

"What about the poachers who are after you?"

He smiled. "All the paperwork and reports I'd been turning

in had actually identified the ringleader, the youngest Messick brother, or make that a half-brother, who worked at the department and was the resident mole. He had a different last name. By the time the dust is settled, all the arrests will have been made. I do have to pick up Horse, who probably thinks I abandoned him at the vet. I… I'd be glad to drop you off wherever you'd like to go."

"That won't be necessary. The police—Detective Hargrove—said he'd take me home."

"I'm not sure you want to go there. They haven't found wherever it is that they took all your furniture."

She frowned. "I'm sure they will soon. And you have to get back to work—"

"Not really. I'm out of a job now."

"Oh, I'm so sorry."

He grinned at her and her blush deepened. "No to worry. My brother, Boone, that I told you about, wants me to open up an outfitters operation in the area. I can stay at my place and work out of there."

"Well, that's good, then." She bent over Izzy and fussed with the dog's ears.

"Very good. So I had an idea. I was going to get a new sleeping bag for Otis and thought you'd like to go with me to give it to him. Something less…odorous." He watched her carefully for any reaction—hoping, praying she'd agree.

"That's thoughtful of you. But won't he be mad you arrested his brother? I mean, weren't they all involved?"

"Nope. I guess they weren't the sharpest at keeping a big operation secret, so were never a part of it. As for Otis, he'll be so excited about the sleeping bag, he'll forget the rest of it."

"In that case, yes. I'd like to thank him as well."

"And then I thought…" He hoped his expression didn't look as desperate as he felt. "Until you either get your things back or get new furniture, you might want to stay at my house in Orofino."

"So Fish and Game doesn't own it?"

"My grandparents did. It's mine now, or will be when I finish transferring title."

"Really?" It came out as exhaled air. "I…that's…that's… thank you." Her voice cracked. "I wasn't sure…everything seemed so…"

"I know. Maybe you'll let me come by and visit sometimes."

"Yes. I'd love that. I love…" She looked straight into his eyes. "I thought I'd pushed you away. I was so stupid, Joshua. I didn't mean it—about just being friends. I was scared, and I didn't know how to say what I really felt."

His heart seemed to stop, then started again, faster. He crossed the room and knelt in front of her, taking her hands in his. Her fingers were cold, trembling, but they curled around his like she was holding on for dear life. "I'm not going anywhere unless you tell me to."

Her eyes searched his. After a moment, a soft smile spread across her face and her eyes sparkled with unshed tears. She leaned forward until her cheek was pressed against his. He could feel her breath against his skin, warm and unsteady. "I don't remember everything yet, but every moment with you is engraved on my heart. I love you." Her words were so quiet he almost missed them. "I don't know how to do this, with Ruth and everything else, but I do love you."

The world stopped. The walls he'd built around his heart tumbled. He'd prayed to be able to feel again, to be seen as a person, not as a man with a scar who needed to be avoided. He wanted the moment to last forever. He leaned away and brushed her hair off her cheek. Slowly, his hand drifted to the dog tags he wore, the metal cool against his fingertips, heavy with memories of battles fought and losses endured. He unhooked them, the faint clink of the chain sounding louder than it should in the quiet room. With a reverence he hadn't felt in years, he slipped them into his pocket, as if shedding a piece of the armor he'd worn for too long.

"I love you too, Bethany. And we'll figure it out—together. Ruth, the investigation, all of it. You're not alone."

Izzy shoved her way between them, her tail smacking his leg, and Bethany laughed. It was the first time he'd heard her laugh with that carefree mirth since he'd met her.

They both stood. Bethany's hand found his and she laced her fingers in his. "I'd say I'll pack up to go, but I don't seem to actually own anything." She looked around the room. It didn't matter. Right now, with her hand in his and Izzy sprawled across their feet, nothing mattered.

This was enough. She was enough. And he wasn't letting go.

* * * * *

Dear Reader,

Thank you so much for joining Joshua, Bethany and Izzy on their adventures! You might also enjoy meeting Boone—Joshua's brother—and Amanda in *Escaping the Wilderness*.

I placed this adventure south of my home in North Idaho in a little-known region of the country. I've been blessed with tackling the white water rafting on the Lochsa and Clearwater Rivers and enjoying the breathtaking scenery of the area.

I chose a bull terrier as my canine heroine for this story—a breed I've owned since 1989. I am well acquainted with their funny and unique temperament. Though my main breed is Great Pyrenees—I'm an approved American Kennel Club judge—you'll always find at least one dog in my books.

I always love to hear from readers and book clubs. Feel free to reach out to me on my website: https://stuartparks.com/carrie-stuart-parks-home-page/. While you're there, don't forget to sign up for my newsletter to keep up with all my news on new releases, forensic and fine art, and, of course, the doggies. On Facebook you'll find me lingering at CarrieStuartParks.

Much love,
Carrie